PRAISE FOR BRETT PETERSEN

If George Bataille and Ray Bradbury had a baby,
and that baby was GG Allin, and that GG Allin
baby read Ursula K. Le Guin and Charles Bukowski
in equal measure, and that now grown-up baby
watched Beavis and Butt-Head reruns on summer
afternoons, then we might approach describing the
phantasmagoric mise-en-scènes Brett Petersen has
put together here in this collection. The contact high
one gets is contagious.

— DANIEL NESTER, AUTHOR OF *HOW
TO BE INAPPROPRIATE*

A Confusion Wave beaming in from the farthest-out
Far Out, scrambling up to unscramble our partially-
scrambled minds.

— BEN LOORY, AUTHOR OF *TALES OF
FALLING AND FLYING*

Stories in the wheelhouse of Jeremy Johnson,
Harlan Ellison and Phillip K. Dick. These are really
fucking cool.

— GARRETT COOK, AUTHOR OF *A
GOD OF HUNGRY WALLS*

Petersen's stories are an acid-drenched, kaleidoscopic blend of genres reminiscent of Dick and Burroughs, but with their own unique breed of genius. The experience of reading *The Parasite from Proto Space and Other Stories* is not unlike ingesting a powerful psychedelic—one that will leave a lasting impression of your psyche.

— BRENDAN VIDITO, AUTHOR OF
NIGHTMARES IN ECSTASY

Reading *The Parasite from Proto Space* feels like you're on a footchase pursued by Mad Mr. Petersen himself. He's got a messenger bag full of creatures he spliced together in his basement workshop, and every time you think you're getting ahead, you turn around to check if he's still behind you and get smacked in the face by a 50-pound alien memory worm that needs you to validate its childhood trauma.

— CHARLENE ELSBY, AUTHOR OF
HEXIS

Buckle up because you're about to be thrown into a wonderfully distorted reality. Brett Petersen's collection invokes the excitement of reading Bradbury and Heinlein for the first time. *The Parasite from Proto Space* raises important questions what it means to be human and twisted world eagerly waiting to consume us. A must-read for science fiction fans everywhere.

— MAXWELL BAUMAN, AUTHOR OF
THE MUMMY OF CANAAN

This is clearly a parable about being an outsider and just trying to fit into this world. I feel like it's an anthem for most of my generation, whom, now pushing their 40's, are still trying to figure shit out. It's morbid, bizarre, and a ton of fun. Over all it kept my attention. As I'm often to point out, for a reader like me with severe ADHD that's all that matters. Getting me to sit in place and read a full book is extremely difficult and anyone who accomplishes that feet can wear that as a badge of pride.

— REED ALEXANDER, AUTHOR OF *IN THE SHADOW OF THE MOUNTAIN*

THE PARASITE FROM PROTO SPACE

& Other Stories

BRETT PETERSEN

CL◀SH

CONTENTS

A MESSAGE FROM THE AUTHOR

This book is dedicated to those on the autism spectrum, those with mental illness, and those with disabilities both visible and hidden. My advice to you is to never stop pursing what makes you happy. Your path through life may not resemble what your aunt, the so-called experts, or well-intentioned but misguided friends have in mind for you: and that's perfectly fine.

Around the time I received my bachelor's degree in English, my mind was hijacked by a dangerous parasite called the Typical American Career Path. Its only goal was to steer me away from my writing, music and art, and mire me in a dead-end janitorial job that didn't pay nearly enough for me to move out of my parents' house. I entered the work force a college graduate with an ear-to-ear grin and the determination to earn a living. Two years later, I was wheeled out on a stretcher and into an ambulance bound for the psych ward.

Everything changed when I started collecting Social Security benefits and moved into a subsidized housing unit a block away from my favorite record store. That's when I began to recognize the parasite's influence and take action against it by channeling all my energy into my creative passions rather than what society expected of me.

Like many autistic people, I was born with a handful of finely-tuned skills. Pragmatism, the most valued trait an American citizen can possess, was not one of them. I write songs, draw crazy cartoons, read Tarot and write books, but I simply don't have what it takes to drive a car, work a traditional job and live the quote unquote American Dream.

In the words of my grandmother, every person's ultimate goal should be to become 'actualized.' This entails pinpointing your calling, chasing it like the Holy Grail, and never letting anyone (or thing) knock you off course. It doesn't have to be a career in literature or the arts: it can be anything! If your grail is gainful employment, then trail it like a bloodhound.

This book is my most earnest attempt at self-actualization. It is one of the few things I can give to this world. These nine stories chronicle the dreams, nightmares, visions, and real events I experienced through the parasite's compound eyes. I sincerely hope these tales will give you the strength and courage to shake off your own parasites and pursue actualization. Embrace your eccentricities like loved ones and follow them wherever they lead. Any internal or external stimulus that tries to drag you down is just a parasite trying to get in. Simply tell it to fuck off (through medication, meditation or whatever method works best for you) and continue on your way.

THE PARASITE FROM PROTO SPACE

"This is the story of three girls trapped in three different towers," Jamie, owner of J-BaL's (Jamie's Bar and Lounge) said, swinging the microphone cable around his head like a lasso. The high from the KFC (ketamine, fentanyl, and crack) injection was nearing its climax. His words made about as much sense as a message hidden in tuna footprints, but that was the point of shooting KFC. The audience was hooked on it as well; one needed to be high on Colonel in order to enjoy the insanity that often went down at J-BaL's open mic night.

"This is also the story of a man," Jamie continued, "a boy really, on a quest to rescue the girl held prisoner in the highest tower. The two other girls are okay in his book, but the boy's heart is fixed on his prize: the feather-haired beauty with chlorine eyes. Her tower is the most fortified structure known to man: a titanium spike piercing the pink pillow clouds of planet Palumphagus ... otherwise known as Detroit, Michigan. Its entrance is guarded by bioroid tanks that could shoot down the La Gracia Orbital Colony if need be. Rescuing her by air is impossible due to the energy shield generated by a machine humming in the basement of a nearby church. That church is where the hero of this story trips on a wire and unplugs the shield generator. This is where the story is supposed to begin. But let's not begin it there ..."

Someone in the audience belched, scenting the air with onion mist.

"In my opinion, it will suffice to start where all the action is ... the epic ka-booms! and ka-blangs! of the *climax* where the hero dodges lasers and missiles, rescues the girl, and takes her home and fucks her. But that's not what happens at all. Nope. Not even close. As you'll see, this story is not derivative of your typical Hollywood action thriller. There may be goblins and frost-giants smashing McMansions with their clubs, but none of the characters care. You know why? Because writing from a stance of boredom and passivity is much less cliché than making characters actually give a shit about the fantastic elements thrown in to appease the author's nostalgia for sci-fi and fantasy. Eventually, passive narrators will become old hat both in and out of academic circles. Casual readers and students will doze off as plots become predictable, and professors will be susceptible to fits of rage knowing that their home city isn't producing literature of remotely good value.

"So, instead of boring you with the same old tropes of princesses developing Stockholm syndrome and knights in white fedoras causing the immolation and combustion of people and objects, I am going to let my very special guest tell you a story inspired by a lump of cancerous matter on the eyeball of a toad yearning for something to yearn for. There will be no desperate soliloquies of longing for fame, glory, money, pussy, or cookies ... just pure, unfiltered linguistic aberrations that exist solely to cushion the psychological bludgeoning resulting from weaning one's self off of moonshine. What you're about to hear is a verbatim transcription from the mind of a telepathic tonsil stone hacked onto a monkey's face by a hawk with undescended testes. These words are a tonic that needs no gin. Friends, relatives, fuck buddies, and total strangers, I am proud to present to you the story of *The Parasite and his Mission to Save Humanity from the Coming of Proto Space* as told by the Parasite himself. Take it away Mr. Parasite!"

There was some weak applause as the Parasite took the stage.

"Thank you Jamie, for the kind introduction," he cleared his vacuole. "Before I get to the thesis of my presentation tonight, I figure I'll tell you all a little bit about myself. As you folks can probably tell," he scanned the audience with his shiny black eye, "I am not from this world. My neck of the woods is a place where there are no such things as days, feelings, or objects. You can't even call the main body I broke off of a planet, solar system, or even a body at all. It's like a photographic negative of a glob of white-out the size of a galaxy; a planarian that moves through the universe devouring whatever it touches. It is not a black hole. It's much different than that. Proto Space, which is the closest the English language can come to naming it, has been around since the beginning of ..."

"Bullshit!" An empty beer bottle sailed past the Parasite's head. "Who do you think you are, pullin' this sensical crap on us? Do you know where you are, pal? This is Colonel Country, motherfucker! We come here to shoot KFC and listen to lit'rature that don't make no sense. We don't wanna hear none of your straightforward narrative shit, you hear me?!"

"Sir, I'm sorry, but ..."

"Fuck you!" Several figures rose from their seats and began to file out of the bar. "Lousy prick!" Someone spit in the Parasite's direction.

"Alright then," Jamie took the mic. "Let's hear it for the Parasite, everybody!"

One person clapped. It was a thirty-something man in gray sweats. His belly shook like a sandbag as he smacked his tiny hands together. He was probably the guy who burped before.

The Parasite slunk offstage and into the bathroom, slamming the door behind him.

Sensing that the night was pretty much over, Jamie tied a shoelace around his arm, plucked a fresh syringe from his belt, popped the needle into a vein and pressed the plunger. Divine utterances coursed through his bloodstream until they found their way to his tongue. He knew that if he kept talking, the Colonel would descend from on high and transform his ramblings into poetry or, if the drug was quality; a coherent narrative. As Doug the Pusher always reminded his clients; KFC makes sense of nonsense and vice-versa. It will fuck you. You need it in order to live. I'm your supplier. My word is Gospel.

Jamie grabbed the microphone. "Later that night," he made a face like two skunks had crawled up his nostrils and had sex in his sinus cavity, "the Parasite lay in bed smoking a stogie found in a nearby ashtray. His girl lay beside him, her arm wrapped around his carapace. She was a college student he had met while bar hopping the previous weekend. She didn't make enough money as a burlesque dancer to pay her tuition let alone maintain a steady supply of cigarettes. The black orb in the center of the Parasite's face looked sad and moist as he stared at the ceiling.

"It's okay, baby," cooed the girl, her shoulders softened by the cotton of her shirt. "I'm sure you'll get it up next time. We just need to try something new in bed, that's all."

He'd had the confidence of a bull moose when they first met. What had happened? At what point had he let his guard down and allowed self-defeatist thoughts to creep in?

"Like what?" he sniffed, "we've tried everything; anal, oral, nasal. Just because my dick is made of Proto Space doesn't mean I can do *everything*. I guess I need to be all there mentally before I can make you happy," he groaned.

"It's because of those jerks at the bar, isn't it?"

The girl traced one of his spikes with her finger.

"Just ignore those fuckbags. Everyone's allowed to give a crappy open mic performance once in awhile, right?"

"B-but," the Parasite's lower mandible was trembling, "it's just that I don't think anybody cares about the coming of Proto Space or the fact that I can guide them to Post-Space, which is a much better alternative. Salvation is right in front of their faces and nobody gives a fuck!" The Parasite grunted and smacked his skull with his spiked claws.

"Stop that!" the girl became cross. "You just need something to boost your confidence." She tossed onto her left side and clicked off the lamp. "I'm going to bed. Maybe something will come to you in your dreams, I don't know. We'll talk about it in the morning."

"Good night," the Parasite croaked, but she was already out.

The next morning the Parasite awoke to find the girl missing. Had she gone to class? Not likely, since it was summer break. Did she have a job? Maybe she went to the gym? Then reality sunk in. She had left him for a creature much younger and more physically fit. The Parasite stared up at the bumpy white ceiling. Life in this dimension was grinding his brain into powder. It made him not want to get out of bed ever again. If only he could curl up under the blankets and disappear into a pocket universe: preferably one where no one could find him. Maybe he could find a way back to Proto Space where he belonged.

His mission on Earth, however, was his top priority. On December 28th at 11:41 pm, the region of space housing Earth and its solar system would be devoured by Proto

Space. The Parasite hadn't done a very good job of convincing people to go to Post-Space though. His appearance frightened most humans. Sporting several thousand legs, a black orb for an eye, and a spiny exoskeleton, it was very difficult to get people to listen to him. He'd made efforts to boost his popularity by performing at events such as the open mic night at J-BaL's, where everyone was fucked up anyway, but it was to no avail. Simply put, he was a loser. Even back home in Proto Space, he wasn't the most amorphous, the most incomprehensible and nowhere near the most eldritch. He might as well assimilate back into Proto Space and reunite with Grandma and Uncle Kmkwlggh and every other parasite who had cast aside their individuality out of boredom with corporeal life. That way, he'd be a part of something powerful and all-consuming despite no longer having a personal identity.

"Fuck it," he shouted at the bare walls. "If I can't convince people to seek salvation through Post-Space, I'll just become part of Proto Space again. As far as humanity is concerned, Proto Space will be an upgrade from this hell hole they live in."

He reached for his cell phone to check the time. It was already 4:30.

"Fuck," he rolled onto his side.

The scent of the girl he'd been sleeping with for the last seven nights was still on the sheets. Strawberry rain. He liked that smell. Not too overpowering; a perfect complement to the scents of sex. But now she was gone, and so was the sex. Oh well. He kicked off the blankets and sat upright. The apartment smelled of impotence and failure. What was he going to do today? His mind began to wander. What am I doing with my life?

He earned his keep by selling vials of Proto Space as a street drug. The only piece of furniture he owned was a bookshelf. None of the books on his shelf were of Earthly origin. He had brought them from home; books written in his mother tongue on subjects completely incomprehensible to the human mind. One such book, translated at the expense of most of its meaning, was titled *The Cellular Regression of Sheep Over Water*. He pulled the book next to it from the shelf. This one was titled: *An Arboreal Light to Unlock Nothingness and Parasouls*. He flipped through it. One of his legs landed on a sentence halfway down the page:

"The mysteries of sloth exit stage left while fires beneath the ocean illuminate the Abacus breathing life into the End of Time."

Even he couldn't understand it. He sighed.

"Well," he crawled out of bed head first like he used to when he was a child, "time to get on with the day. I think I'll go to the mall. Yeah! That's what I'll do. I'll check my bank account balance and then maybe I'll go to MATCH! Video Games (More Addictive Than Colonel, Homie!) and see if they've got anything new. I could even get a patty at Bock Quacky's Chicken and Duck Burgers! Should I get chicken or duck? I guess I'll flip a coin."

The Parasite scuttled across the bedroom floor, picked up a musty t-shirt and smelled it.

"Eh, smells clean enough," he donned the shirt, careful not to further tear the holes his ex had cut into the fabric for his spines. He brushed his mandibles, downed some Proto Space with a glass of water, gathered his phone, wallet, keys, iPod, and backpack with his laptop in it and headed out the door and down the stairs to the air conditioned lobby. He checked his mailbox: nothing except for that Shop-Rite coupon he'd kept in there for weeks. Oh well. He selected the album 'Planetary Duality' by the band The Faceless from his iPod and went off into the residual mugginess of early September.

———

He didn't find anything at MATCH! Video Games. He chatted with the clerk for awhile about games, anime, clowns, and hypothetical scenarios involving rooms full of headless mannequins. But as always, the subject eventually turned to the fate of the universe.

"So, what happens when matter is assimilated into Proto Space?" The clerk's eyes were wide with mock curiosity. Normally, humans had no interest in talking about Proto Space or its implications. But this grunt-level salesman who sold 'retro' electronic games, toys, trading cards, and other collectibles to autistic thirty-year-olds, – a job akin to waving insulin in front of a diabetic's face – was enough of a dork to humor the Parasite. Every other day, the Parasite would shuffle into the store and browse the same old shelves in search of Japanese Role Playing Games to play on his days off from missionary work. Since JRPGs were rarely traded in and the Parasite had nothing better to do, he'd stand by the register and prattle on and on to the clerk about how Proto Space was good, but Post-Space was better and blah, blah, blah, et cetera, et cetera.

"Well," the Parasite scratched his eye with one of his facial claws, "it goes something like this: when Proto Space makes contact with matter, it accelerates its entropy. It causes the particles of whatever it touches to run in fast-forward. Proto Space will eventually spread across your entire universe and everything will be reduced to nil. This is the Fate decreed unto you by our race. However, there is still a chance for humanity to achieve a state of bliss even more ideal than that which Proto Space offers."

"And, how do I achieve such a state?" The clerk smirked.

A little boy and his mom entered the store. The boy began to jump up and down at the discovery of a plush Bullet Bill.

"By allowing me to guide you to the Paradise known as Post-Space," said the Parasite. "Post-Space is a world without trauma, turmoil, strife, pain, decay, or death. It was built for all who seek refuge from the harshness of the physical world as well as the false paradise of Proto Space. Although Proto Space is a reprieve from mortal suffering, arguably a step-up from the conditions of your reality, it is still not ideal. It's like entering a perpetual state of Zen. No good, no evil, just Existence for its own sake. Post-Space, on the other hand, consists only of what humans call 'goodness.' Post-Space is a luxurious carrot cake with cream cheese frosting whereas Proto Space is a sheet cake from Walmart served in a church basement. One is obviously the better choice, but both are food and contain sugar and carbohydrates."

"What is our reality here then?" The clerk glanced around the store to see if any customers needed help.

"A can of diced chicken cubes and gravy from the bargain shelf of a grocery store in a low-income neighborhood." The Parasite couldn't help but snicker.

"Fair enough," said the clerk. "In that case, I suppose it doesn't matter whether I choose to go with you to Post-Space or remain here and get sucked into Proto Space. I'm not much of a cake fan anyway. I think I'll just chill here in Space-Space and enable people with shopping addictions until the Fated Hour arrives."

"That's your call." The Parasite shot a glance at the little boy who was now bawling because his mom refused to buy him a two hundred dollar comic book.

Since his arrival on Earth in the year 2001, the Parasite had been prescribed psych meds to numb the distress of the human condition weighing him down at all hours. His doctor was Edmund Jeffries, a man who had dealt with much more volatile clients that the Parasite. Jeffries often expressed his opinion that it didn't matter whether humans chose Proto or Post-Space. The Parasite's job, he argued, should be to educate people about the existence of Post-Space while allowing them to choose their own destiny.

"That's one way to look at it," the Parasite approximated a smile.

"Yes, and isn't it comforting to know that some might view the Walmart cake as a special treat in and of itself? If one is always seeking a better piece of cake, how can one ever be satisfied? I mean cake is cake. I'd be happy just to have a piece of cake at all," Jeffries chuckled in his doofy way and flashed the Parasite a buck-toothed grin.

"You're starting to sound like my mother," the Parasite tried with all his strength to keep from scowling.

"Now, tell me something about your mother," Jeffries was unabashed. "You haven't said much about her. Did you two have a good relationship?"

"Uh ..." the Parasite's left mandible began to twitch, "I guess so. I mean all of us Parasites, my brothers and sisters that is, were born from the dark matter core of Proto Space kinda like how a mushroom spore splits off from its parent."

"I see," Jeffries began to scribble on a sheet of yellow loose leaf paper attached to a clipboard. "Does it bother you that someday you'll have to return to your mother, that is, to where you came from?"

"You mean like when I assimilate back into Proto Space, like when this universe is completely taken over? Yeah, it's something all Parasites worry about just as humans worry about death. This thing you call 'death', by the way, is no big deal to us Parasites. We know exactly what happens to a consciousness when its body stops working. It ain't bad at all."

"What happens when humans die?" Jeffries bit the

eraser of his pencil with his pursed upper lip, one of his many quirky mannerisms.

"They become part of Post-Space, which is probably the biggest reason why nobody wants to go with me; because they would be literally volunteering to be killed. Nobody wants to die, but that's just because they have no idea what awaits them after the fact. They say stuff like 'but I don't wanna die, I just wanna stay here and live out the rest of my life and die naturally,' which is total bullshit. Things will get better for them no matter what they do, but there are only three months left before the arrival of Proto Space. When that happens, everyone on Earth who isn't already dead will be locked out of true salvation forever. If only they could see just how golden the opportunity is that I'm offering them. Everyone's argument seems to be that they need 'proof.' 'Prove to me that the reality you preach about will be better than the one I'll end up in if I just stay here,' they say. What I want to say to the fuckers is 'how can I prove something so monumental to an organism content with eating cubed chicken and Walmart cake for the rest of eternity?' It's as though I'm offering a deer tick an ocean of blood and it refuses simply because it can't understand how to pay the entry fee to the beach club. All humans have to do is trust me ... it's as simple as that, but no. They see me as some kind of monstrosity from outside of time who wants to rob them of their free will and goad them into shedding their individual forms and become some kind of one-body, one-mind pot of human soup. I guess that's technically what happens when a human assimilates into Post-Space, but it's like learning to drive a car. Once you're over the threshold of fear it just feels natural. Not that I've ever driven a car ... but maybe I should learn just to prove to you humans that Post-Space is not so bad."

As the Parasite spilled his guts, Jeffries continued to jot.

The conversation meandered to the college girl and back

to Post-Space again before Jeffries glanced down at his watch and signaled that their half-hour session was over.

The Parasite crawled down from the pleather chair with the brass buttons. Jeffries bid him farewell and shut the door behind him. The Parasite figured by the time he got to the drug store, his prescriptions would be ready for pickup. He navigated the labyrinthine corridors of the medical office building with his keen memory of the building's layout. His eye was capable of seeing in 360 degrees as well as a multitude of possible timelines for living things and objects. It took a lot of strain on the Parasite's part to utilize this type of sight. It was akin to a human straining their eyes to read the fine print on a medicine bottle. The Parasite was several millennia old, a twenty-something in human years, but he was already beginning to feel elderly.

Two months went by and still, nobody agreed to be 'chaperoned' to Post-Space by the Parasite. After each appointment with Jeffries, the Parasite would visit his local drug store and pick up his prescriptions. It was nearing the end of December. The Parasite had all but given up on his mission. If the human race was content with mediocrity, then they didn't really deserve to be saved. The Parasite figured he'd stay on Earth until the day before Proto Space usurped the cosmos. Perhaps he could bang one more State University floozy before all her emotional highs and lows became a perpetual flat line. While waiting in line at the drugstore one day, he got an idea.

Though he was certain he couldn't contract human diseases such as the flu, he decided to get a flu shot anyway since his pharmacist, a lady with a certain girl-next-door-ish quality about her, had offered. Maybe he could convince her to get coffee with him before Proto Space rendered all coffee flavorless and transformed laughter into a ubiquitous hum.

———

Abigail Mazurowski, the pharmacist, beckoned the Parasite into a tiny office and offered him a seat in a plastic chair.

"Hello," said the Parasite, feeling friendlier than usual. "I don't believe we've ever spoken for more than a few minutes."

"I think you're right," she chirped, smiling a smile that could've melted a glacier on Pluto.

"It's nice to know that I have such a cute pharmacist."

"Aww," she cooed with perhaps a hint of bashfulness, "why thank you. Now which arm ... or ... leg would you like your flu shot in?"

"Any one is fine," the Parasite's eye landed on a pack of Depend undergarments as he glanced around the room.

Abigail opened the syringe kit, dipped a piece of cotton in alcohol and swabbed one of the fleshy parts of the Parasite's forelegs. "Okay," she said, "just a little pinch."

The Parasite winced at the cool fluid being pumped into his leg. The coolness radiated throughout his upper body, encasing his head, his midsection, and then his entire body in an icy tingle.

"Feels good doesn't it?" Abigail smirked.

"Yeah," said the Parasite. "I didn't know flu shots could feel *this* good."

He felt like he was in one of those York peppermint patty commercials, standing on a mountaintop. Then it was like he was standing on the surface of a frozen moon in some region of space untouched by starlight for several billion years.

Wait a minute. The Parasite wiggled his legs. *What the fuck? I can't feel my legs, my face, anything!*

He cried out, but he wasn't sure if his vocal appendage had delivered the sound. Ice was ringing in his ears. Then came the voice ... Abigail's voice ... reverberating like the call of an Arctic explorer off the walls of a cavern: a shrill, metallic echo.

"I thought you might like a taste of what you've been offering people all the time you've been on Earth. This is what happens when an organism born from Proto Space makes contact with Post-Space."

Is she serious? Since the Parasite's speech apparatus didn't work anymore, all he could do was think. *What is she? Could she be ...*

"I can hear your thoughts and yes, I am a Parasite like you. My goal is to quelch Post-Space awareness in this dimension by snuffing traitors like you. The coming of Proto Space is the best thing for this universe as well as every other. Goodbye now, I hope better things await the particles that constituted you once they all dissipate and become free energy."

The Parasite was beyond speech. How had he not been able to predict this unfortunate turn of events? How could there have been another Parasite roaming the Earth this whole time without his knowledge? Perhaps his fifth-dimensional sensory organs were deteriorating. It was too late to ponder the hows and whys at this point. His frozen body was breaking into smaller and smaller pieces. Memories were slipping out of his head and swirling down a space-time sinkhole. Could there potentially be a better life awaiting him on the other side of ducks and garbage and geese and honk? Honk! There goes Doug the Pusher on his bicycle again, past the tomato shop where Wallace and weapons and cane and horse plow can't shut mother plck stich   chumsklu&9jf9jfikpo8djpasjiaeji>>>>>>>gasentry wool nomes end game stigelo bilgoum ... aaand ... that's all for tonight, folks!"

Jamie placed the microphone back in its holder. "Hope to see you all next week. Let's give it up once again for the Parasite from Proto Space!"

The man with the sweatpants and the onion breath clapped. Everybody else had left.

"Where did he go?" Jamie glanced around the room.

"He went to tha shitter like twenny minnits ago but hasn come out yet."

A ball of ice formed in Jamie's gut. Usually, when people went to use the shitter in this joint, they never came out alive.

Jamie crept slowly up to the door. He wrapped his gangly fingers around the handle and turned it slowly.

The sweatpants man sat in his chair picking his nose. He watched as Jamie opened the door and went inside. As soon as Jamie's slender form disappeared into the murky shadows of the shitter, the door slammed behind him.

It wasn't until five or six minutes after the sweatpants man had flicked his booger that he became concerned about Jamie. The emcee had been in there an awful long time, and he was the only one who knew the location of the sweatpants man's car keys. The man got up from the plastic chair and adjusted his underwear, which had gotten pinched between his butt cheeks. As he plodded over to the shitter, he noticed the telltale signs of a hangover swirling in his brain like black static. He knocked on the door.

"Jemeh?"

The man had lost his ability to annunciate years ago.

"Y'in ther?"

Something like fear scuttled across his heart.

"I'm com' in okey?"

He turned the doorknob, which felt like one of Frosty the Snowman's testicles. As the door creaked open, a gust of frigid wind punched him in the face. Flurries of snow eddied into the nightclub. The man stepped through the door and into a shin-deep drift of freshly fallen snow. The door no longer led to a bar bathroom. Beyond the door was a winter wonderland filled with candy canes, pine trees adorned with colored lights and a house decorated with wreaths and cardboard cutouts of reindeer pulling Santa's sleigh. The cars in the driveway looked old-fashioned, like they came from the late eighties or early nineties.

The man trudged through the snow toward a window lit by a single candle. He wiped away the frost with his bare hand and peered in. Sitting on the floor next to a Christmas tree and mountains of presents were three small children. Their parents watched over them with mugs of cocoa sitting on the armrests of their maroon leather love seats. The parents were beaming: vicariously reliving all the holiday joys they experienced as kids.

The sweatpants man hiccuped.

He began to feel slightly less drunk.

"Boy," he said to himself, "musta bin some strong shit Jamee put in my Long Guyland ice tee," he hiccuped again, "I dun eevin feel drunk no more. I feels like, I cud geddoff booze atlagether when I'm in this place."

He smiled and noticed his teeth were chattering and that he couldn't feel his legs.

"I bedder get me someplace where I ken warm up."

All at once, the snow began to melt. In its place, a wooden floor emerged. Walls and a fireplace sprouted from the ground and a roof formed over his head. Then he saw that he was surrounded by old friends. Jamie was there, as well as all the friends that had disappeared from his life when he became an alcoholic. That was after his wife Anna had died of breast cancer. The place looked awfully familiar. Then he remembered; this was the Christmas party where he and Anna had first met. If his recollection of events was correct, she should be over by the table with the white cloth dipping a piece of shrimp into cocktail sauce and talking with Ralph Henderson, his former coworker.

He shuffled hurriedly past Jamie, who patted him on the shoulder and offered him some eggnog, to which he said "no thanks." And there she was: Anna Elfman, the lady with high cheekbones who used to leave sticky notes on his cubicle wall with caricatures of their boss on them. Anna had been an art major in college, but had resigned herself to becoming a middle manager for a printing company when she hit a wall of student loan debt after trying to sell her art in New York City.

When he approached her, the scenario played out exactly as he remembered it: déjà vu. Except he was now one hundred pounds heavier and dressed in clothes swiped off the free table at St. Vincent's Thrift Store. Experiencing this moment again conjured up feelings akin to those of the parents in the other house reliving Christmas through their children's eyes. Although nothing in any universe ever remained the same for long, new experiences could resonate with old ones and become all the more sublime. When nostalgia mixes with the exciting, trailblazing quality of new traditions, it's like having your cake and eating it too. And the cake tastes amazing whether it's from Walmart, Trader Joe's or a grocery store in a low-income neighborhood.

This new universe in which the sweatpants man found himself: a universe made up of Post-Space as opposed to Proto or Ordinary Space, would never repeat itself. It would remember the past, celebrate the present, and maintain high hopes for the future.

The sweatpants man, now clad in a white tuxedo with frills and a bow-tie, kissed his wife-to-be and continued to kiss her for as long as he wanted the moment to last. In Post-Space, any given moment had the potential to last forever. But when it was over, it could only return garnished in the dressing of a new memory, just as potent as the old, carrying the hope of infinite new ones to come.

SUMMONING THE MEMORY EATERS

The cardboard trees surrounding Bethlem High School discharge several dozen volts of electricity. The current travels along a fence until it reaches a basketball hoop where it creates a portal. A mealworm the size of a dog wriggles through the portal and plops into a puddle of rain water. It slurps up the memories of a ninth grade girl who fell into the same puddle 2,340 years ago. A tether ball swings in the breeze as the worm slithers along the soil collecting bone fragments, bug carcasses and other detritus with its mucus. It detects the ghosts of bipedal beings who once ran across this field kicking rubber orbs, sweating, breathing, laughing and contemplating their futures. Once upon a time they were nymphs in bloom, blessed with countless years ahead of them. The worm senses that things are different now.

The year is 4444 and everything is dead: unless radioactivity counts as life. The worm inflates a nodule on one of its sides. This nodule approximates a sigh. This particular species of extra-dimensional mealworm does not experience emotions like most creatures in its neck of reality. They can imitate empathy if it gets them food. Their diet consists not of other life forms, but of abstractions such as thoughts and memories. To the worms, the haze of melancholy coating this world tastes like vanilla ice cream chased with Bailey's.

Once every 2,222 years, the worm colony from the dimension-next-door sheds its collective skin and merges with the Perpendicular Line to form the Great Ellipse. To molt, the worms require large amounts of a chemical created through the metabolization of ideas. The best sources of ideas are places where sentient races have had technological breakthroughs followed by mass extinctions. Over several billion years, the worms have evolved the capability to traverse dimensions in search of these locations.

If the worms do not molt, they will be unable to merge. The Line will reject them if so much as a micron of dead skin remains. Merging is the worms' best defense against the Inverted Wolf Fang: top predator and guardian of the Vanishing Point at the end of their universe. The worms feed their old skin to the tooth-beings who live in quantum pockets inside their imaginary limbs. The tooth-beings excrete enamel and the worms smear it on their bodies to protect themselves against the Wolf Fang's gamma rays.

Next time you have a brain fart and can't remember where you put your car keys, consider this: the reason people forget is not because of memory retrieval error. Forgetting is the result of extra-dimensional mealworms from the future eating the memories stored in your ghost. These ghosts contain all of the memories accumulated during their respective bodies' lifetimes. What happens to your ghost in this era affects your former body retroactively. For instance, if a worm were to take a bite out of the memory of the time you fell off your tricycle and got a boo-boo when you were three, you might misremember various details. *Was the trike blue or red? What is a trike anyway?* If a memory is consumed entirely, it ceases to be. The worms mean no harm, but if they succeed in devouring every single human memory, it will be as if we never existed.

Ghostly forms blanket the courtyards of Bethlem like the flu inside a hospital in February. The worm devours their memories in a matter of seconds. It will have to return home soon because the time of molting is drawing near. It oozes over a rusted sprinkler jet and onto a plateau of asphalt. Parked in rows are fleets of yellow sentinels forever watching the school entrance with unblinking eyes. Perhaps their lids opened and closed long ago. An image of their windshield eyes blinking enters the worm's field of perception. It has picked up a visual from the ghost of a boy boarding and disembarking the sentinel like a wooden doll on the rails of a cuckoo clock. The worms can see memories as well as eat them, but they make no attempt at interpreting or understanding them. It is simply an evolutionary mechanism like a bat's sonar. A bat doesn't consider an insect's point of view; all it wants is a tasty snack.

◙ ◙ ◙

2,430 years ago, Bethlem High School was a center for mediocre public education. Students shuffled through sweaty hallways, sat in seats, scribbled, listened and scribbled some more. They attended P.E., ate hollow chicken nuggets, scribbled and listened and went home. No one ever noticed the presence lurking behind the walls: millions of quivering, segmented tubes waiting to burst through and gorge on juicy adolescent reveries.

No one except for me.

When I worked as a substitute teacher's aide at Bethlem, I came to appreciate too late the beauty of youth that tarnishes with age. Each day, I understood more and more what had been taken from me and what was continuously slipping away. The kids would understand it in due time. As soon as growth stops, decay takes over. Soon, the whole world would succumb: the walls would crumble and everything would be inundated with doubt, cynicism and worms.

I remember sitting in class with a student on a Monday afternoon. Though his social skills needed a lot of work and some of his behaviors made me cringe, he still had something I didn't. The teacher wrote math problems on the dry erase board. To me, they looked like random squiggles. I'll never figure out how I passed the Regents exams when I was in high school. This kid I was supposed to be assisting who peeled dead skin from his lips in the middle of class was living far better than I was. He was *free* in ways he wouldn't realize it until it was too late and he began to decompose.

He raised his hand and asked to go to the bathroom. I escorted him and waited outside the door. I breathed in the dusty air of the hallways. The tang of fruit-scented shampoo and body spray took me back to my most cherished nightmares.

At that time, I was a recent graduate of St. Vincent's English program. Every night, I would dream about signing up for a high school class just for the hell of it. Despite the work ethic I had cultivated in college, I would end up failing the class. How and why my dream self decided to enroll in a high school class as a mid twenty-something, I'll never figure out.

My student exited the bathroom and I walked him back to class.

The teacher managed to squeeze in two-and-a-half more problems before the bell rang. The halls became alive again with teenage laughter and drama.

A thousand more worms spawn from the basketball hoop. They're everywhere now. They're appearing in other places besides Bethlem: St. Vincent College, Moon Island, Beginnings Preschool, Endings Retirement Home, Gramma's house, the patch of grass at summer camp where I became aware of death for the first time and even the snow-covered porch where I found out that Santa Claus wasn't real.

If I were to define my current state, I would say I am a ghost that has retained its self-awareness. I have yet to encounter another like me. Don't ask me how I got this way. All I know is that this whole thing started 2,430 years ago. It was the last day of school at Bethlem. I had gotten in a verbal altercation with my father who had been a teacher there for thirty years. I ran out of the building and into the woods where I tripped and hit my head on a rock. While I was unconscious, I had a vision of a clock hand spinning and pointing at reversible geese, potpourri qubits and other quantum anomalies. When the hand stopped, it landed on a number that didn't exist. The number unfolded like a paper crane and became a calendar page marked '2222.' I figured that must've been the year I was being sent to.

When I regained consciousness, I was in the same woods, except everything was gray and dusty and the trees were made of cardboard. The air was crackling with radiation and worms were everywhere. I tried to cut one in half, but all it did was split it into two separate worms. After hacking at it for hours, creating a thousand tiny worms, I concluded that they were harmless.

Over the course of a millennium, I figured out how to reach into their heads and extract their 'thoughts.' Not only did I learn where they came from, how they ate, survived and reproduced, but I discovered that I was immune to having my memories eaten. It must be that for a worm, trying to eat the memories a sentient ghost is like a biting a titanium-plated apple.

At the dawn of this century, a question I had never considered began to nag at me. Was I the one who caused the apocalypse and summoned the worms? I'm not positive, but it might have been my longing for the past combined with the emotional outburst in front of my dad and hitting my head on that rock that caused the hands of Heaven to crank open the portal and let the worms through. These same hands snuffed out humanity and tossed my ghost 207 years forward in time. Could being stranded on an empty world as a consciousness without a body be a punishment from God? The apocalypse ... triggered by me ... all because I couldn't stop thinking about youngsters in harnesses, swinging on ropes, joking and dreaming about going to college, hallways that kept me alive, kept my heart fresh and vitalized.

The worms are all over the world now. It is the same as it was 2,222 years ago. They're crawling up the steps of the Capitol building to feast on the fancies of the Founding Fathers. They're climbing into the orifices of the Eiffel Tower to dine on Derrida's *différance*. They're lapping up the legends of Terra Cotta Army soldiers. They're scarfing the campfire stories of tribesmen in Africa. They're dancing around teenage banshees sitting cross-legged on the volley-ball court contemplating suicide. They're preparing for the Merge. I hear the tooth-beings rattling in their imaginary cavities like lottery numbers. Their atoms jiggle along to the chime of school bells. 4:44. Has the fated hour finally arrived?

I feel the Inverted Wolf Fang rotate 180 degrees and prepare to plunge into the spongy membrane of the dimen-sion-next-door. The worms cock their heads toward the West. The enamel harvest has been interrupted. The tooth-beings honk like injured geese. The worms experience a fleeting flicker of worry, but they let it slide and resume their consumption of psychic morsels.

◙ ◙ ◙

The school bells ring for the thousandth time. No, it's my alarm clock! I jolt out of bed and check my phone. 4:44 a.m.? Sweet, I'm up nice and early for a change.

I heat up some soup, eat it, brush my teeth and take the pill I was supposed to take last night. My head is gonna feel foggy all day because I screwed up my sleep schedule with diet Mountain Dew and crappy novels about human cloning written by some fuckhead from America's heartland. Oh well. I just hope that when I take the same pill tonight, it doesn't turn me into a fiend clawing at the walls of my bedroom or a shrink-wrapped pallet in a warehouse where emotions soil everyone's lives with coffee shits and bad breath germs; where there aren't enough mops in the world to clean the insults I spouted at that guy who worked at the Distribution Center.

I take the bus from Thrushcross Mall to the Heldeberg Valley library. It is the same library in which I spent hours reading Joyce, Faulkner and Austen only to fall asleep after two pages. As I open a Word document and prepare to write, I begin to wonder if I'll ever have a job again. Believe me; I *am* trying to cope with life now that the structure of school has been lifted from my chest like a chunk of Adirondack granite. Will I be able to gather the work ethic to plow through the edits on a story I wrote back in 2008 about a boy haunted by a particular species of bird?

The answer to that question is moot because in *reality*, it's the year 4444 and I'm a sentient ghost watching the human race's memories being eaten by worms. I sigh and imagine my throat swelling up like a worm's when it finds it necessary to mimic emotions like sadness. Sometimes I like to imagine I was never a terrible person. What did I want to be when I grew up? No one in 1995 would have thought 'janitor' was a good answer. That's one of the things I did before I worked at Bethlem. Thank Heaven I found the courage to sleep on the job that day and get fired. After two weeks in the psych ward and three of putting CDs in boxes at the Distribution Center, I landed the job at Bethlem. It was the only job I ever enjoyed. But like every other good thing to come into my life, it was temporary. I remember wanting to be a teenager again so badly. Sometimes, I would forget I was twenty-five and my psyche would regress to that of a seventeen-year-old learning about DNA, Apartheid and the motivations of Holden Caulfield in *The Catcher in the Rye*. The only problem was that many of the female students looked like adult women. I had to be extremely careful about where my eyes landed while glancing casually around the room.

I suppose I was jealous of how few responsibilities these kids had hanging over their heads. The little fuckers had the power of 20/20 hindsight at their disposal; hindsight gleaned from the failures of *my* generation. Learn a trade. Don't bother enrolling in an expensive private college. Get a two-year degree at a community college if you must, and immediately enter the work force as a cook or roofer. Whatever you do, don't study the arts or humanities: it's a trap!

Even the student I worked with who picked his nose in class and got in peoples' faces like a cartoon animal ended up having a better future than me thanks to the trials and errors of us millennials. I hope you're enjoying your existence as a blissfully unaware hologram, kid.

As soon as I think this, twenty-five-hundred worms spill out of a stop sign and plop onto the gravel. This brings to mind a haiku a friend once read to me:

> *How was I to know*
> *That my actions during life*
> *Would kill mankind's ghost?*

> —Fomo
the Japanese poet whose only fear was of missing out.

The bell chimes one final time. Every worm on Earth begins to vibrate. They spread their forms outward and gel into a single entity. Satiated on memories, the worm-sphere tears a hole in the fabric of space-time with a bolt of lightning. It separates from the Earth and floats through the hole which zips itself closed.

Back in its native land, the worm-sphere coils around the Perpendicular Line and becomes the Great Ellipse once again. The Ellipse sheds its skin and the tooth-beings slurp it up. With their bellies about to burst, they void their bowels in unison. The Ellipse extends a feeler, scoops up a dollop of enamel and rubs it all over its body. The survival of the Ellipse and the tooth-beings is ascertained for the next 2,222 years. As for me, I will continue to exist as a ghost on a dead planet, lamenting the passage of my high school years for the rest of eternity.

BILLY-SALLY

A bright light streaked across the sky and disappeared into a thicket. Billy-Sally the billy goat glanced up from the grass he'd been munching on. Something on the other side of the fence was glowing. He padded cautiously to the edge of the pasture. The glow danced on the surface of his eyeballs like Chinese lanterns above a lake. The urge to jump the fence and investigate tugged at him, but Farmer Alan would be very cross if Billy-Sally were to try. Perhaps he could sneak through the front gate when the cows were let out to be milked.

Billy-Sally waited. The sky went from purple to black. Finally, the gate was opened and the cows ambled toward the barn. Billy-Sally darted across the gravel road and made a bee line for the thicket.

After extruding himself from fistulas of bramble and vine, Billy-Sally reached the source of the glow. Resting in a crater of flattened shrubs was an orb of light so bright he couldn't look straight at it. Regardless, the thing beckoned him to touch it. When he finally summoned enough courage to nudge it with his nose, he found it cold and smooth. When he withdrew his snout, the glow stopped.

As soon as the spots of green and blue faded from his corneas, he saw that the object was a silver sphere with a panel in its side. He backed away. What if a coyote were to spring out and slash his throat? He felt like running, but something commanded him to stay. The orb had the same shiny surface as Farmer Alan's truck. Could there be Cheeto crumbs strewn across its floor?

Before Billy-Sally could make a move, the hatch hissed white smoke and slid open. A translucent, purplish mass oozed out, gathered around Billy-Sally's hooves and enveloped his whole body. As it entered his nostrils, he could smell the blue water from the bottle Farmer Alan sprayed the cow-stalls with. Billy-Sally felt sleepy. It was as if he was being loaded into the old cattle trailer with some fresh hay for a trip to a faraway place.

When Billy-Sally came to, he was in a valley of magenta beneath violet spires taller than the tallest mountain. Tree branches bursting with kaleidoscopic veins clawed at a sky into which a black hole had been burnt by a cosmic cigar. The hole sucked in any two-headed dodo birds or bat-squirrels that flew too close. The city on the horizon was a domed megalopolis populated by humanoids wearing bubble helmets and puffy suits. Titans in business attire lumbered across fields of iridescent anemones, sipping black espresso and chatting with each other about work, taxes and other such grails of existential discourse. Droplets dribbled from their chins, scalding the ant-people forced to live in earthen mounds by decree of the Super-Computer who ruled over the dome-dwellers and therefore, the world.

Blades of wormgrass smeared their mucus on Billy-Sally's hooves. Chunks of pretzel-wire fell from the under-gills of mushrooms towering fifty feet above him. He curled up beneath a mushroom and began to tremble. He felt as though an invisible hand had seized his stomach and was trying to drag him into a realm of ice and fear. Was this feeling normal for a billy goat to have? Did it matter? The only thing he could think about was getting out of there. He stood up, began to trot, gallop, stampede. He kept stampeding until he ran into something and got knocked out.

When he regained consciousness, he was lying on a hard surface. A bright light blinded him, and all he could hear was the whining of drills and the beeping of computers. The silhouettes of masked men and women loomed over him.

"What we have here is an extra-dimensional, uh, creature that has crossed the boundary from Y-22b into our own Z-14c," said a man.

"M-hm," a woman on the other side of him replied.

"It is not clear how this happened," the man continued, "but hypotheses have been floating around regarding the Skyhole which has been growing in size ever since the appearance of the Inter-Dimensional Mealworms."

"To be honest, doctor," the woman cleared her throat, "I don't think this has anything to do with the Skyhole."

"What do you suggest then?"

"I don't believe it would be a stretch to say that the creature just *appeared* in our dimension for no particular reason. Phenomena without cause are rare, but they do happen. Take the beginning of the universe for example. Something springing from nothing is the best explanation we have as to how existence came to be. What we have here is a one-in-quintillion instance of a being from a parallel world slipping into ours by means unknown."

"Duly noted."

Billy-Sally heard scribbling pens and metal scraping metal.

"Alright," the doctor fished a pair of latex gloves from a

dispenser and snapped them over his hairy hands, "I think it's about time to get started with the vivisection of this wonderful specimen who had the misfortune of wandering into our laboratory today."

Nervous laughter fluttered through the room.

"My hope is that this individual can provide us an example of a taxonomy that could only come to be in a universe with different laws of physics."

Your life is in danger! A voice deep within Billy-Sally screamed. *You must escape immediately!*

He didn't know what the words meant, but something about them injected the urge to run into his muscles. He leapt from the table, knocking over trays of surgical knives and darted through a hallway past two shrieking women in bubble-suits. He was being pursued. He had to find a way out as soon as possible. There was a loose ventilation grate in one of the walls. He knocked it aside with his horns and crawled in.

Several minutes went by. After the shouts and footsteps faded, he felt it safe to venture out and find a better hiding place. He noticed a green door across the hall that had not been there before. He smelled something yummy wafting from beneath it, so he went in.

The door swung open and Billy-Sally found himself in a forest that smelled of pine and cooked meat. In a clearing not far off, green and blue deformed humanoids sang and danced around a lamb roasting on a campfire. Billy-Sally tried to sneak past, but knew he had been spotted when a bulb-headed one pointed a stubby finger at him.

"Oodgka bodgka lee laah?" it grunted.

Billy-Sally cocked his head.

"Ooskabba leeba lah! Ooskoinchka eedgka aah!"

The rest began to chant and jump up and down.

After several minutes of jumping and chanting, one whose nose was a prickly pear approached Billy-Sally.

"Skamooch yeb haigh," it snorted, "lagbafrechel beh ybusk. Oom shlaign eho hurrrrgh!"

"Hurrrrrgh!" the others responded.

Billy-Sally couldn't understand, but sensed he was no longer in danger.

"Schnaig blaigh, horchkum," said one whose skull was shaped like a pyramid, "skrum nub higwuffle?" He made a flapping motion with his hand.

"Aigh! Higwuffle! Higwuffle!" The others flapped their hands as well.

Billy-Sally didn't know what to do, so he drew two intersecting squiggles in the dirt with his hoof. The squiggles happened to form the Hebrew letter Aleph.

The tribe gazed at the Aleph in awe. Their eyes began to blossom with stars and galaxies. They were being shown secrets of the cosmos that no other race had the innocence or dumb luck to stumble upon. A spark leapt from the fire pit. Ripples of Holy Light tore through the forest. The subtleties of the message might have escaped the simple woodland dwellers, but a loose connection in their puny ganglia had been rewired. A current of Gnostic Revelation flowed where before there had only been stalagmites of dried boogers.

A vision of moths with white-hot angel wings holding hands with pine cones entered Billy-Sally's mind. They waltzed to the tune of a song he remembered. Where had he heard that song? Something told him that both the song and this moment of Gnosis would soon be forgotten. He closed his eyes and lay down next to the fire which had simmered to glowing embers. He dreamed of a void in which a pixel blipped in and out of existence in a fraction of a second. As he slept, the wind blew away the Aleph he had drawn in the soil. The tribe drank mead from sheep's horns and laughed all through the night.

Billy-Sally awoke the next morning to a milky sky and dunes stretching to the horizon. The forest and the tribesmen were gone. Before him was an infinite desert, but somehow the clouds in the sky were comforting. They told him that rain would soon come. As he stood and shook sand from his back, a clap of thunder sounded. It began to drizzle, rain, and pour.

As he trudged through the wet sand, fronds of foliage sprouted beneath his hooves. The fronds grew taller as he walked. Eventually, they grew so large that it seemed the forest had grown back. But something was different. This wasn't the coniferous forest in which he had slept the previous night. There was something unsettling about this humid, dank jungle.

As soon as the trees had completely grown back, Billy-Sally noticed empty stone temples everywhere. He thought he heard the sound of drums too: an infernal banging like a migraine throbbing against the back of his eye. If he wanted anything, he wanted to go back home to Alan and the day-to-day rituals of farm life. He wanted reality to be consistent; not an amorphous dreamscape which was never the same from one moment to the next. Why had he decided to check out that glowing object in the thicket next to the pasture? He didn't know. He had never questioned the motives of his actions before. Why should he start now?

Wait a minute, he thought. I'm questioning the motives of my actions? Since when do I do that? What is 'I' anyway? Am I, I? I suppose I am, aren't I? I am ... Billy-Sally. I am ... a goat ... an animal ... I am *not* a human ... but what is a human? Aren't they animals like me? Farmer Alan has referred to me as both a goat and an animal before. What is the difference between a goat, an animal and a human? If humans are *not* goats *or* animals, then what are they? Are

humans human because they know that they are themselves? If that's true, that must mean *I'm* human ... because I
know that I am I!

He looked down at his hooves. They were black and
caked with mud. He found a puddle of rainwater and
studied his reflection. This is *my* face, he thought. It belongs
to *ME!* I am I, and I am also me. I look different than a
human. My face is long and my eyes have black rectangles in
them. I have horns and humans don't. I have hair all over my
body. Humans only have hair on their heads and arms. Am I
the first goat, the first animal, the first non-human to discover
that I am myself? If so, that means I'm different from all the
other animals on the farm now. How did this happen? Is it
because I came to this place?

The questions just kept coming like the rain pattering on
Billy-Sally's back. He had to get out of this jungle and find
his way home. First, he decided he should find somewhere to
spend the night. Luckily, there were ruins all around.

After about half a mile, Billy-Sally found a structure
with a roof. He shook the water from his pelt and found a
mossy place to lie down. There was a block of stone in the
center of the pavilion. It was some kind of container with a
lid about the length of a human body lying supine. Could
someone be sleeping in there? Billy-Sally had to find out for
sure. He got to his feet, walked over to the box and nudged
the lid with his snout. He pushed and pushed, but it was no
use. It was too heavy. He stood on his haunches and concen-
trated all of his force into his front legs. With great effort, he
got the lid to budge a few inches with a grating sound that
made his flesh crawl.

Before Billy-Sally could catch his breath, a steaming
mass of tar, bristles, ocular appendages, ovipositors, feelers,
and mandibles spilled out of the box. It made a sound like a
tumor wagon slamming its brakes.

———

After running for half an hour as fast as his legs could carry him, Billy-Sally sensed he was nearing the edge of the jungle. He felt relief even though he knew in all likelihood; he'd be thrust into some other random setting again by the logic that governed this world. He was tired of this. He wanted to go home, eat some pellets and grass and be petted by the neighbor's children. He wanted to fall asleep beneath the familiar, old stars. The old days never got younger. This, Billy-Sally reasoned, was a universal law.

As he approached a clearing, he saw something up ahead running toward him. It was another four-legged creature. Was he seeing things? No. This was definitely real. As he moved closer, he realized that it was his reflection again. He raised his hoof and the other Billy-Sally raised his. He touched the other Billy-Sally's hoof and found it to be cold and smooth. The edge of the jungle was in fact, a plate of reflective glass. He'd once heard Alan's wife Martha refer to such an object as a mirror.

How was he supposed to get out? He thought about it for a minute or two. Perhaps the only way out was *through*.

"Wait a minute," Billy-Sally spoke aloud. "I know what this is! This is what humans call a metaphor."

All at once, his synapses lit up in a fireworks display replete with angels blowing trumpets and Merkabah descending and grazing the barrier of the lower world with its gilded wheels.

"Breaking a mirror is symbolic of destroying one's conception of self," Billy-Sally continued. "In order to escape this world, I have to reach a higher level of consciousness by destroying my animal self. The simple pleasures of farm life were sufficient for the old Billy-Sally, but now I realize there is no turning back. The broken shards of the mirror will probably kill me, but my death is necessary for the birth of a new Billy-Sally: one who is not only self-aware, but who has the potential to know things unknowable by humans. In my next form, I will solve all the great mysteries and even uncover new ones. I will be the greatest being that has ever lived. My mind will be like that of God. I may even *become* God and direct the consciousness of all living things toward a state free of evil and suffering. In a matter of two or three generations, I can save the universe! I will do what Jesus and Mohammed couldn't. I will bring existence to its logical conclusion: peace and happiness for all!"

Billy-Sally backed up ten feet and counted down from three. On zero, he sprinted as fast as he could, head down, poised to smash the mirror that lay between him and universal salvation.

Upon impact, the mirror shattered. Shards of glass sliced his face, cut through his eyeballs and punctured his brain. The sharp, pixelated world beyond the mirror moved at half the frame rate Billy-Sally was used to. He found himself suspended in an amniotic sac that was also an iron maiden. He felt the pop of a vacuum nozzle piercing the sac, preparing to abort him. Death's hand collapsed his wind-pipe. His serotonin levels tanked. Old synaptic connections were being severed. Rerouted. Alzheimer's. Forgetting things. Trivial details. Corn mush. Sweet taste. Noontime? Treasured memories. Mother's teat. Cold outside. Brothers and sisters. Half moon. What color were they?

As more and more information leaked from his head, he began to feel comfortable; like the receptors responsible for alerting him of physical and emotional pain were being frozen off. It was a soft, drifting feeling. He didn't mind it. In fact, he liked it. Then there was nothing to like ... nothing to dislike ... there was just existence ... then existence itself ceased and the world went blank ... a blank infinity swad-dled in blankets of nothing ... a butterfly disappearing into itself ... silence ...

———

On January 11th 2015, Martha gave birth to twins at Saint Peter's hospital in Albany New York: a boy and a girl. As the newborns squirmed in her arms, she and Alan named them. The boy was Billy-Sally and the girl, Sally-Billie. Alan pointed out that both babies had birthmarks on their foreheads. Billy-Sally's was shaped like an Aleph and Sally-Billie's resembled Tav, the last letter of the Hebrew alphabet.

Alan took pride in having the smartest goats in the nation. His most famous goat Billy-Sally had been a first prize winner four years running in competitions the held by the American Goat Society. Unfortunately, the goat had run away sometime in April. Alan had led search parties, but Billy-Sally was never found.

One of the searchers uncovered a silver orb in a thicket of trees adjacent to Alan's property. There had also been stories floating around among the townspeople of cattle going missing and strange lights in the sky. But Alan didn't pay these rumors much attention. It was probably just coyotes or something. The orb, Alan reasoned, was a prop built by local kids to stir up an extra-terrestrial hoax.

THE LABYRINTH AND THE JINGLING KEYS

Some nights when I can't sleep, I carve stories and poems into the walls with a chipped-off piece of the white material that cages us. They are inspired by the altered realities I experience while asleep. These realities are created by drugs dissolved in the water. There are no pills, so it has to be the water. What other explanation could there be? I mean, I haven't had a normal dream since I arrived here twelve years ago, and the dreams always seem to happen right after I drink the water they give me every night in a paper cup. You might not believe me when I say this, but I actually look forward to the dreams. In the dreams, I'm always floating in a Sea of Black with all these bubbles containing different realities I can enter and participate in. More often than not, the bubble-realities are better than my waking reality. At least they inspire me to write, unlike the puzzles and mazes they put me through all day.

Tonight will be one of my writing nights. I dig out the sharp piece of white stuff from under my mattress and carve an anecdote I thought of today:

"Getting up and waking up are two different things."

I like it, I decide.

I glance at the digital clock embedded in the wall: 10:04, it says. I don't feel tired yet, so I continue to scribble. Maybe I'll write a little bit about the history of my being in this place in case someone new ever moves into this room, so they will be able to know who I was and where I came from. Hopefully by reading it, they won't feel as alone as I did. Here goes.

The last memory I have of my parents is an ugly one. They have just dropped me off at this place and it is time for them to leave. Dad is peeling mom away from the door. She is hysterical and in tears. Her sobs become quieter and quieter as dad drags her out of the building. Then I am all alone.

Before the tears can come, two ladies in green uniforms lead me through a big white rectangle and undress me. They take me to a room where a hundred other boys are huddled together naked. A voice on the loudspeaker says there is going to be a mandatory shower. The hot water stings my skin and the steam makes me thirsty.

After the shower, they dress me in an olive green shirt and pants and lead me to the intake room. After they measure my height and weight and examine my body, they show me to my living space. The tiny room has white walls, a bed, toilet, sink, washtub, mirror and clock. I never see any of the other boys again. Where do they keep them? I wonder about this for years afterward. They have to be here somewhere.

I don't sleep at all the first night. It takes all the strength I have to keep from crying, from thinking about home. Then, before I know it, the morning buzzer farts in my ear like a fire alarm. A lady with rotten fish breath enters my room.

She fits me with a black vest and walks me to the Central Area.

There, waiting for me, are bins of blocks. Blocks! I'm excited. This is going to be fun after all. I dig my arms into the bins, grab handfuls of blocks and listen to the *clack, clack* sounds as they fall. Then an image of a block tower appears on a screen across from me. The voice on the loudspeaker tells me to build a tower just like the one shown within ten minutes. I try my best to do what it says, but I don't get it right in time. Something stings me like a million bees and I fall to the ground crying. The voice tells me to rebuild the tower.

"It hurts," I sob.

Another burst of pain. I feel warm urine pooling beneath me.

"Rebuild the tower!" The voice commands.

"No!"

More bee stings.

This goes on for hours until I finally realize that if I do what they say and do it as fast as possible, there won't be as much pain.

Then, finally! I get the blocks in the right order within the time limit...but then it's on to the next assignment.

"The next assignment?" I pout and stomp my feet.

If I whine or throw a tantrum when I'm supposed to be putting shapes into holes, they shock me. If I stop listening when they want me to find a red triangle at the end of a maze, they put me on lockdown.

Lockdown is where they hold you down, wrap you up like a mummy and stick a tube up your nose and down your throat that hurts and makes you cough and choke every time they do it. Then, they pull your pants down, swab your penis and behind with something cold and slide tubes in that hurt even worse. Then they bring you to a closet, hang you on a hook, turn off the lights, lock the door and leave you there until you stop crying. When you've been good long enough they let you out. But if you're only just pretending to be good, they know right away and send you back to lockdown. They know because they monitor your thoughts and actions with hidden cameras and sensors.

Over the course of the next twelve years, I learn that there is no use in fighting. Doing what they say and enduring the shocks is a much better alternative than getting tubes shoved up your nose, dick and asshole. Having reached age sixteen, I've become conditioned enough by the constant trial and error to do exactly what they say and to do it right the first time. And even now, with hair on my pits and privates, I don't always get it right the first time. And when that happens, which it sometimes does, I bash my head against the walls over and over and over. I can usually get in about five good bashes before they discover I'm self-injuring and either shock me or put me on lockdown. It's not as if they care about my physical well being. They don't give a shit about that; they just don't tolerate any behavior outside of the Code of Conduct. The Code of Conduct is as follows:

1. All tasks must be completed within the allotted time.

2. All clients will receive eight hours of sleep or leisure time.

3. Engaging in any activity other than assigned tasks during allotted time will result in punishment.

What the Code doesn't say is that we are rewarded for completing these tasks with food and water. This makes me wonder; what is the importance of all this? What purpose does this facility serve? Perhaps it has something to do with the drugs they give us; the drugs that cause those bizarre dreams. Could they be testing the effects of the drugs by making us run mazes and solve puzzles? Are the dreams induced intentionally or are they just side effects? What do these drugs really do? Maybe they're doing it for no reason at all. Maybe the people who run this place are just a bunch of dicks who find pleasure in using their arbitrary authority to torture us.

As I put down my writing implement, I notice the familiar feeling of a switch being turned off in my brain. Sleep will soon be upon me. I yawn. Tonight I'll have good dreams, nothing grotesque or horrific.

I find myself in the Sea of Black again. I'm dreaming, I realize. As always, the Sea is tasteless and odorless.

Bubbles, some of them larger than houses, appear at the fringes of my peripheral vision. One of them contains a gingerbread house on top of a hill of powdered sugar. In another, a young soldier is lying on a cot. Flies are swarming around a spear of bone jutting out of his leg. A second soldier is pouring whiskey down his throat and a third is sharpening a hacksaw on a slab of stone.

Yikes! I swim as fast as I can away from that one.

Some of the others, however, look quite desirable.

There's one in which a bunch of cartoon characters are racing go-karts on the surface of a glazed donut. In another, a nude woman is lying on a couch and a man, also nude, is serenading her with his basso voice. There's even one where a talk show host is doing tricks on a pogo stick. Every member of the audience has his face and they are spraying the air with silly string! I can't help but chuckle. There are a lot of crazy bubbles in this area. I see one with a dog eating brownies out of the hands of a mime with the eyes of a fly.

What the hell? A bunch of bombs falling on a sepia-toned landscape superimposed with footage of a hooded man laughing? I shudder. I think it's time to move on to a different region.

After swimming awhile and seeing nothing, I sense a new one about to rise from the depths. Call it a sixth sense, but something tells me this one is going to be good.

As the bubble surfaces, I gaze through its glossy skin. It contains image of me seated in a plush chair staring at a television screen. A bag of corn chips is crumpled up on my lap and my chest is dusted with crumbs. A lazy afternoon of doing nothing but watching TV and eating corn chips? I grin devilishly.

Sounds like the best afternoon anyone could ask for.

I swim up to it, extend my right leg and dip my toes in. Then my foot, leg and entire body gets pulled in as if the bubble has its own gravity. I'll never get used to the feeling of the membrane sealing around my head.

The air inside is stuffy like someone had just jerked off and fallen asleep during a porno movie. I settle into the chair and reach for the remote control and the chips. Before I can press a button or bring a handful of chips to my mouth, ribbons of coarse material wrap themselves around me. I struggle against the straps, but they're too tight. I can't breathe. I scream for help but I can't hear my own voice. A pair of mechanical claws emerge from somewhere behind my head and hook themselves beneath my eyelids, prying them open. Thankfully the claws drip with some sort of saline solution to keep my eyeballs moist. If I wasn't under such stress, I would remark as to how cleverly this device was designed. The TV clicks on; its antennae quivering like the feelers of a chrome cockroach. To my disdain, it's reruns of *Seinfeld* again. This happens sometimes. The drugs take something that would seem benign and harmless and turn it into a torturous, hellish experience.

Seeing George Costanza shove shrimp in his mouth for the eleventh time, Jerry make his six hundredth joke about sex or airline peanuts, Elaine do her autistic shaman dance and Kramer burst through Jerry's apartment door on an endless loop, I come to realize that this is the *only* reality I will ever know.

After twenty years or eight hours of intertwining situational comedy plotlines segmented by slap-bass and the forced laughter of the studio audience, morning arrives. The clock on the device sitting below the TV says 7:30, but to me, time has ceased to exist. *Seinfeld* has ended and *Everybody Loves Raymond* has come on in its place. The actors and sets are different, the plots are different, but the mechanical laughter of the studio audience remains the same. Thirty five years gets crunched into half an hour. Time becomes a neutron star so dense that it slurps off my skin like whipped cream through a straw. My body becomes the chair, the chair crumbles into dust, the dust disperses throughout the Sea and the Sea collapses in on itself, revealing the fact that it is simply another bubble within a larger, much emptier Sea.

As my mind disassembles itself in an attempt to comprehend the void and the voids within voids beyond those voids, the world flickers off with that strange sound analog TVs make when the screen goes blank. The claws release themselves from my eyes and the straps retreat back into the chair. I rub my stinging eyes and massage the sore spots on my lap and torso where the straps had dug into me. Chips are scattered all over the place and the bag is nowhere to be found, but I am finally free to leave the bubble. Sometimes, I feel like these bubbles aren't just fragments of my subconscious floating up from some unknown depth. Sometimes I am truly convinced that whatever reality the drugs tell my brain is real *becomes* my reality.

I feel a gurgle rise from my belly. Maybe I can find a bubble with some food in it. I swim toward the edge of the little room where I can see the outer surface of the bubble wavering iridescently. I stick my hand through, then my arm, shoulder and head. The membrane feels cool against my neck and upper torso, like I'm bathing in a pool of spring water. I wriggle myself free of the bubble's gravity and begin to search for one containing either food or at the very least, something interesting.

Awhile later, I come across a section of the Sea that I recognize. This is where those jingling keys are, the ones that surround a certain bubble I've been trying to get to for years. Those damn keys. I shudder. The one time I almost made it to there, the keys started rattling so loudly that I thought I might go deaf. And for weeks afterward, all I could hear during my waking hours was the metallic clanging of those keys, a noise like migraine hallucinations of metal rakes scraping my brain. Never again, I told myself. It's just not worth it. I do an about-face and swim toward a different bubble teetering on the edge of my left periphery.

I do the breast stroke for what feels like hours without finding food. Finally I reach a bubble that seems intriguing enough. The object it contains is an ornately-adorned, golden vacuum cleaner with "Dirt Devil" stenciled on the bag in blue ink. My gut is growling, but this is too interesting a find to pass up. I simply must have this device for myself.

I stick my fingers into the bubble and savor the cool, watery texture of the membrane. Then I insert my hand, my arm, and suddenly my whole body is sucked in and the outer surface seals behind me with a little *boop!* I contemplate the golden work of art before me. The bag is woven from silk and the head is solid gold and studded with sapphires and lapis lazuli. I examine the cord, also gold, and notice that the silver prongs have been unplugged from the wall. Out of pure curiosity, I insert the prongs into the outlet and press the ruby button on the side of the head. The vacuum roars to life, and in an instant, I regret having activated the thing. Its suction is so powerful that it swallows the bubble and me along with it.

Buzzing hornets assault my left ear. I swat at them but they don't go away. A horizontal white line splits the Sea in two. The line thickens and the blackness retreats like twin curtains. Beneath the curtains are the familiar whiteness of the Room and the red glow of the Clock. It is 7:30 in the morning and the buzzer is sounding. My bed is damp with sweat and I'm still here in the facility. Fuck! There is a crusty bagel in the slot next to the door and I have only ten minutes to eat it before it is time to run mazes and solve puzzles. I throw off the covers, leap over to the slot, wolf down my breakfast and chase it with some funny-tasting tap water.

Peering at my face in the tiny mirror above the sink, I see that it looks the same as always. My ears and nose remind me of my parents. My eyes are cerulean like the water of the pond they used to take me to when I was little. That pond was where some of my first memories took place. With a sigh, I recall how we splashed and laughed and played Marco Polo and how the water-jumpers hopped right onto land and ate crackers from our hands. At the end of those long summer days we'd sit together on a grassy embankment and watch the sun setting behind the hills, molten and red like a coin thrown into a fire.

One night on the car ride home, I remember catching a glimpse of my father's eyes in the rear-view mirror. He seemed to be gazing at something far-off. What he said to me then gives me chills to this day.

He said, "It won't always be like this."

My lower lip is trembling. I swallow what feels like a dry marble in my throat. I turn on the faucet and splash a handful of cold water on my face. "I've got to keep plugging." A droplet forms on the tip of my nose and falls into the sink. "That's what Dad would have said if he was here."

The puzzles are as difficult as ever today. I solve one in which I have to raise and lower the water levels of three separate tanks in order to achieve equilibrium. Next, I'm told to reorder a jumbled mosaic of a man wearing a suit and to direct a laser beam toward a statue by repositioning mirrors. After that, they have me stack fifty pound blocks to form a tower high enough to reach a hole into which I am to deposit the egg of a chickipede without cracking it.

Finally, after zig-zagging down the home stretch of a maze filled with guillotines and lava pits, I reach the goal-post, a flashing neon panel with a red button. I press the button and the panel speaks in a salesman-like voice.

"Congratulations, you have just passed your four thousand-one hundred-and-fortieth trial! Your complementary sandwich and mineral water are waiting for you in the slot to your left. Have a nice day."

I snatch the sandwich and Styrofoam cup from the slot. A motor whirs and the panel folds back up into the ceiling. Today it's a tunasaur sandwich. Dee-licious! I pinch my nose, down the sandwich in two bites and chug the water. After twelve years of eating this crap, I have successfully conditioned away my gag reflex.

———

On the way to the next Trial Area, I think about what sort of bubble dreams I'll have tonight. Lately it's been harder to tell which reality is real; the white one with the puzzles and electric shocks, or the ones encased in those bubbles floating in blackness. I may even be in a bubble right now and not know it. Once you're in the Labyrinth, I suppose, sleeping and waking bubble-realities become impossible to distinguish between.

Bbbbbrrrraaaaapppp! The buzzer derails my train of thought. The salesman voice says there's been a change in my schedule. I am to report to Trial Area Ω immediately.

When I get there, I am briefed for my next assignment. I am to run a maze in less than five minutes while avoiding spongy orbs fired at me from hidden cannons. If an orb touches me or if I fail to reach the goalpost in time, I will be punished and required to start over. Okay! I spring to my feet, hop up and down, stretch and shake loose my arms and legs. It'll be just like all the other times. I can do this.

The starting gate opens and I take off sprinting, dodging orbs on all sides, leaping over ones rolling along the floor and ducking and tumbling to avoid ones coming from above. I flail my arms and act drunk, trying to make my movements as unpredictable as possible. I jerk to the left. *Whoa!* I do a somersault. *Missed me!* I lunge to the right. *Haha!* Spastic bursts of energy. *Whoops!* Not out of breath yet. *Oh shit!* Almost there. *Oh god!* I can do this. I turn a corner. *Bamf!* An orb collides with the back of my head, knocking me to the floor.

"Fuck!"

No.

This can't be happening.

I'm on the ground. The shocks are singeing my body hair.

It hurts.

Fuck.

I failed.

How could I have failed?

I'm too old for this.

I grunt and rise shakily to my feet. I can't let them see me cry.

Too late.

I'm crying.

I see two female staffers, a brunette and a blonde, bounding down the hall with mummy wrap and cath-tube in hand.

No, no, no, this isn't what's happening, this isn't what's happening.

"I didn't mean for this to happen!" I yell down the corridor at them.

"Get down on the ground!" the brunette shouts.

"No!" My face is burning hot. "There's no way I could've avoided that orb!"

They flank me.

"You gotta let me do it over. Please! I'll get it right this time, I swear!"

They're looking at me as if I'm livestock.

Something compels me to swing at the brunette. I miss and she bars my arms in a full nelson while the blonde spikes my arm with a syringe.

I holler and try to wrestle myself free, but I should know better. Resistance just makes them squeeze tighter.

They bring me to the ground.

"Alright now, you know the drill," says the blonde,

"we're gonna cath you, okay?" as if I'm not aware of the pain that is coming.

"No!" I sputter, saliva leaping from my mouth.

The brunette holds my arms while the blonde, pinning my legs with hers slides down my olive-greens. My flaccid penis pops out and flops to the side. I watch her eyes as she studies it.

"I'm gonna apply some cool gel and you'll feel uncomfortable for about ten seconds, okay? And once we get your cath, feeding tube and colostomy set up, we'll bring you to lockdown where you'll be nice and comfortable, sound good?"

My brain sends an impulse to trigger an erection as she swabs me with cool gel, but I can't seem to get it up with the catheter looming.

"Here it comes, ready, 1...2..."

On three I nearly bite my tongue as pure pain snakes its way up my urethra. My toes curl, my fingers seize, yet, I am somehow able to find a sort of masochistic pleasure in this. Thankfully, the effects of the injection kick in by the time they insert the butt and nose tubes. I'm in a complete daze as they tighten the mummy straps around my body and wheel me to the lockdown closet where I'll hang there like an IV bag dripping piss and shit for two, maybe three weeks.

After what feels like formless, interminable eons of screaming and drooling on myself in the darkness, something suddenly clicks. I feel okay. In fact, I come up with a great idea for a story. The story would begin with a specific image; that of a boy cradling a guinea pig in the hem of his shirt. Perhaps the guinea pig would represent me and the boy would be a knight-in-shining-armor carrying me to freedom. But with a guinea pig brain, I wouldn't be able to see the big picture. My immediate concerns would be my entire world. I would be scared; aware that I was being taken some-where, but not sure where, how or why. What would happen when the boy releases me into the wild? I'd probably get eaten by a coyotebear or ringsnake.

That's when something dawns on me. Something I had never considered before. Could it be that the world Outside is even more fucked up than it is in here? Could this facility actually be protecting us from some greater evil that lies Outside? Maybe. But who's to know? Certainly not me. Like a guinea pig, I'm probably incapable of wrapping my brain around it. At least guinea pigs have the luxury of a short life-span. How long have I lived here? Twelve, maybe thirteen years? That's like three guinea pig lifetimes back-to-back. Guinea pigs have it so easy *and* they're fluffy and adorable. Not like me. At this point, I probably look and smell like a dead body.

Perhaps I *am* a dead body.

I glance at my right hand to make sure I'm not dead. It's veiny and spotted as if it belongs to a person quadruple my age.

"Wait a minute," I open and close my fingers and wave my arm. "I can move again!"

Something about the darkness seems different.

That must mean I'm...

Once again immersed in the Sea, I notice that it is unusually empty. Where are all the bubbles? I scan my envi-ronment, but all I see is blackness. Come on, bubbles. If I can find a bubble, I can at least be somewhere other than the Sea, which is too much like the closet for my taste.

I thrash around like crazy trying to make bubbles appear, but nothing happens. I stop moving and let my chin droop to my chest. I suppose I can float here in peace until I have to wake up and face *true* darkness.

As I lift my head to wipe away the tears, I see something; a faint dot off in the distance. Could it be? Am I saved? I start to swim frantically but realize I have to conserve my strength in order to reach my far-off goal.

The bubbles I encounter along the way are few and far between. There seem to be only clusters of little ones filled with spiders, chocolate wedding cakes, dust bunnies and other pointless objects. What kinds of drugs did they put in my feedbag? I continue to swim, reminding myself that if I get tired, I can simply float there in empty space. It's not as if there's any bottom to plummet to.

I swim and swim until I'm out of breath, every now and then passing a bubble with a ceiling fan or baby doll in it. Something about these bubbles feels uncanny and wrong. They remind me of insects and cancer, tooth shavings and white-hot electricity dancing beneath my eyelids as I'm waking up from a nightmare.

"Nope!" I shake my head violently. "Not thinking about that." I push the bizarre images out of my head and focus all of my awareness on the bubble I'm swimming toward.

I count the movements of my shoulder muscles. 1…2…3… When I reach one hundred and eight, I look up. My target is now the size of a fruit. I can even make out colors within it; green, blue, the deepest, most vibrant red I've ever seen. Somehow these colors seem familiar. I feel my earlier anxieties give way to resolve. I swim onward, motivated by the stunning array of colors within that holy globule. I will reach that bubble even if it takes fifteen years!

I continue to pass other bubbles, most of which contain either clods of soap scum, hair, or nothing at all. Not even gonna look. I breathe in through my nose and out through my mouth. Just gotta keep swimming. I'm only a fish trying to find its school. I've always wanted to go to school. Perhaps there's a school in the bubble up ahead.

I pass one with a little red haired boy spinning the wheels of a toy truck. That's cute. I laugh a little, but feel the emptiness beginning to return. At any rate, I can't get distracted. I have to keep moving.

I swim and swim and swim some more. After seeing nothing but rocks and rusty pipes, I feel doubt trying to pull me down again. Time for another break. I relax and let myself just float there. I wish I could find one with some food or water in it. I'd kill for water that isn't laced with chemicals.

The more I swim, the bigger the bubble gets. My muscles ache, but the mystery of that bubble and its brilliant colors keeps me moving. I train my eyes on it like laser beams. *It* is the center of my Universe. There, I will find what I've been looking for all this time. If I can reach it maybe I can escape from this facility, deposit my consciousness into another pocket of reality far from the puzzles, mazes, drugs, punishments and mind control. It doesn't matter if my body becomes an inert lump and they have put it in cold storage. They can chop it up into a thousand pieces for all I care. The 'me' that matters will be free; free from the constraints of the physical realm, free from medicine, doctors and the powers-that-be, free to exist in an ideal world full of light and laughter and snuggling in blankets. Inside that bubble I will find Heaven; I will shed the darkness like old skin. I will stand beneath the Throne of God, unafraid and willing to accept His love, ready to be enraptured by white wings.

I swim with all my might. Details of the far-off bubble's contents are coming into focus. There is water, grass, a sunset and hills. There are three people swimming in the water.

Oh my God...

I feel as though my heart has stopped.

Could it be?

If this bubble is showing what I think it is, then what awaits me is better than I ever could have imagined.

I squint and scrutinize every little detail just to be sure.

Yes, there is no doubt. It has to be.

It is the pond where my parents and I fed the water-jumpers when I was a kid.

There it is! The holiest of my holy memories is right there, floating toward me in a bubble just like any other. I'm so close I can feel the coolness of the water and the warmth of the sunlight on the back of my neck. I can even smell the piney scent of Dad's cologne as he holds me against his chest. My heart leaps and my whole body flushes with joy and excitement, but the bubble pops and I hear the sound of jingling keys.

THE FUNERAL MACHINE

The Building eats young men and women and shits body bags. I suppose the things zipped up in those black cocoons were human at one point. The bags are loaded into ambulances and taken to some other Building to be incinerated. The ashes are funneled into cheap urns along a conveyor belt. The urns are shipped to the deceased's families, placed on mantles and forgotten. *Time,* working in tandem with machines hidden beneath the floors and behind the walls of the Building, catches all of us eventually. Time moves faster in the Building than it does in the outside world. That's why I try and spend as little time inside as possible.

When I'm out and about and enjoying life, I try not to think about things too much. But sometimes, on snowy or rainy nights when I'm cooped up indoors, my mind begins to probe the dark secrets of the Building. Based on observations I have jotted down in little notebooks while exploring the halls, I have come to the conclusion that the Building is merely a component of a larger system I call the Funeral Machine. Its parts are well hidden, they are disguised as ordinary pipes and wiring. The processes of the Funeral Machine are as follows:

1) The Machine sends nanospores out into the world through its ventilation ducts. The spores alter the DNA of any expecting mothers they come into contact with, causing birth defects in their babies.

2) The defective children do poorly in school and are rejected by the Filtration System designed to weed the Desirables from the Undesirables.

3) Undesirables, declared invalid by the Federal Government are sentenced to one of three places: prison, mental health facilities or group homes for the developmentally/physically challenged. The Building falls under the latter two categories.

4) As a preliminary to being placed in the Building, Undesirables undergo a mandatory full-body examination. Nanomachine injections are administered. At this stage, they are still relatively healthy.

5) As the Undesirables live out their lives in the Building, the Funeral Machine works behind the scenes, firing little lasers and filling tenants' bathrooms with mind and body crippling gas as they shower, (which is the best way to conceal the existence of the gas.)

6) The Machine chews them, so to speak. The tenants become weak, frail and increasingly dependent on staff and caretakers.

7) At some point, after their bodies and souls have been aged and tenderized by the Machine, their vital organs fail and they die.

8) Their inert husks are zipped up and shipped out for cremation.

9) The news media is informed and obituaries are printed. Natural causes account for ninety-nine percent of deaths on the premises, or so the Building records claim.

10) Rinky-dink funerals are held in the lobby. Empty plywood caskets, flowers from the local dollar store and

unmarked slabs of concrete are provided by the Building as

consolation gifts.

11) Generic, pre-written eulogies are read and caskets weighed down with cinder blocks are committed to the earth in an unassuming cemetery in the suburbs.

12) Tears are shed but eventually dry.

13) Life goes on, and the cycle repeats ad infinitum.

Is it naïve of me to hope that I am somehow exempt from being digested and excreted by the Funeral Machine?

The Building has exactly two hundred and forty windows; two windows for each of the one hundred and twenty apartments, twelve apartments per floor, ten floors in all. During the day, the windows serve as the Building's eyes. It observes the comings and goings of people along the city sidewalks. It gazes at them hungrily, waits for them to slip and hit their heads on the ice and become prize game in its blood sport.

At night, the windows become peepholes through which the outside world can observe the inner workings of the Building. Most passersby however, take no interest in the Building. They simply continue on their way: walking their dogs, jogging, going to the store, never giving the Building a second glance. And tenants never dare to venture outside either. For the most part, they don't even realize they are trapped, nor do they have any idea that another way of life exists. Regardless of their cloistered mindset, they know better than to leave their curtains undrawn at night. As soon as the sun sinks behind the hills of the suburbs, they yank their window shades down like a skirt blown up by an undercurrent from a sewer grate. If the ugly truths of Building life were to be put on display, naked for all to see, many residents would likely die of humiliation and shame.

One of the deadliest tactics employed by the Funeral Machine to keep its constituents in line is the spreading of rumors. The rumors are manufactured to distract the tenants and keep them from discovering clues about the Machine of which they are a part. Every Sunday, during the worship service held in the Community Room, new rumors are generated by the Central Computer. The Computer is connected by well-disguised wires to a dummy known as Pastor Raymond O'Doul. Using the angelic-faced O'Doul as a front, the Computer preaches sensationalist sermons laced with misinformation regarding deaths, suicides, murders and burglaries that have taken place in the Building, muggings on nearby streets and sexual predators living in the area.

About a week ago, I heard whispers among the throngs leaving the Sunday service that two lonely old women, shut-ins whom nobody had ever seen or talked to, had overdosed on prescription drugs and died. I couldn't help but wonder whether those two women were real or just made up by the Computer to shift the people's focus away from the outbreak of bronchitis that had sprung up as soon as the new heating system was installed.

One thing I have discovered while living in the Building is that the Funeral Machine's effects can be staved off by engaging in positive experiences with peers: making friends, pursuing hobbies, goals, etc. Although I'm technically a Building resident, I make a point of spending as much time as possible outside. Out there, I mingle and laugh with the City at large, go to heavy metal concerts, drink beer,

converse with kooky people about the Collective Unconscious and vegan cupcakes, recite and listen to bad poetry at
open mic nights. I feel like if I stay in the Building too long,
the lasers, gas and the microbes in the tap water will eat
away my body and mind.

In the past, I've tried to initiate conversations with other
Building residents in an attempt to pull them out of their
dreary world. Despite my best efforts, the opposite always
seems to happen. I get pulled into their rumors and misery
and anxiety. It's as if there's a constant fog of pessimism
hanging over the place. Every time I take a breath, it fills my
lungs and circulates throughout my body. If I remain inside
too long, my skull will become a septic tank and the pus,
mucus, piss and shit will slosh around in there like curdled
milk in a jug.

It won't happen to me, I keep telling myself. Some days,
though, I can feel the Building working on me. I can feel my
skin flaking off, the veins in my eyes throbbing, and my
breath shortening. The moth feelers of the Community
Room TV poke at my heart each night as I sleep.

I wake up with severe back pain every morning. At first I
thought it might be kidney stones, appendicitis or a swollen
liver from drinking too much alcohol while on antipsy-
chotics. Now I'm convinced it's a musculo-skeletal cramp.
The best explanation I can think of is that they've been peri-
odically breaking in and lowering my showerhead, forcing
me to bend over and injure myself in order to wet my hair.
This is just one of many little things they do in order to make
our flesh easier to chew and swallow. There is no doubt that
the Funeral Machine is behind it all.

The Machine consumes everyone eventually, but hopefully

it'll come for me when I'm ninety years old and ready to have my empty casket dropped into a hole and an unmarked slab stuck in the dirt beside it. I may have been born into a wealthy family, but I was never able to acquire the self preservation skills that might save me from the jaws of the Machine. Oh well. At least my children, (if I ever end up impregnating someone,) won't be bankrupted when I pass through the sphincter of this Machine.

One time, this woman who lives in the Building told me that the highlight of her day was being able to walk around the first floor lobby. Sometimes I see her getting picked up by a white van. Where does she go? What kind of life could she possibly be leading? Is she happy? Did she suffer some kind of brain damage? Is she mentally challenged? No, it can't be that. Her belly is swollen as if she's pregnant. If that's the case, I wonder who the father is.

I'll admit that I had a crush on her when I first moved in. We'd stand in the lobby and talk for ten to fifteen minutes whenever we ran into each other. She'd smile, and I'd stand slightly hunched in order to conceal my rapidly inflating hard-on. Then I'd leave, promising to spend time with her at some future point. I never did. I refuse to allow myself to get too close to any of the other tenants. Revealing my heart to them might create an opening for the Funeral Machine to suck me farther in.

I don't know exactly when she became angry with me and stopped smiling when I waved to her. I had sensed genuine warmth in her gaze for awhile. Her teeth were pearly and glistening under the halogen lights when she smiled. She seemed cozy, like her hugs would be an oasis of natal comfort. But somewhere along the line we lost our connection. Was she pregnant, or did she just have a big belly? I don't think I'll ever find out. The Machine will eventually wring the love right out of her like a stained dishcloth, leaving her dry and pale, her tear ducts encrusted with the remnants of tenderness. She will lose her ability to give or receive love. Her flesh will corrode with chemical agents in the Building's climate control system. Her urinary tract will become blocked by too much calcium in the drinking water. Who knows where they take her when she leaves in that van? Maybe she's a corpse kept alive by cybernetics and has to get her augmentations recalibrated. Could that be why I never followed up with her?

Doctors are the Machine's hired muscle. The medical industry keeps us tenants alive but sick and out of the way so we can buy the drugs they manufacture. They get rich. We suffer and eventually die without enough money for a slice of pizza at the local Italian joint.

It should be noted that before I opted to become part of the Machine, I was miserable. I fought every day to keep myself happy and occupied and to keep my thoughts from the darkness that followed me everywhere I went. I had a twelve-ton demon on my back, whispering self-deprecating statements in my ear:

You are not enjoying this.

The fun times you are having will soon end.

You will never again experience the joy you felt as a child.

Nowadays, with 150 milligrams of Olanzapine running through my system 24/7, I find that I'm much happier living in the Building than I was at my parents' house. At least the skin-melting lasers are warm compared to the shards of glass that were lodged into my brain during the years I spent cleaning toilets and mopping the floors of a government warehouse. It wasn't so much a warehouse as it was a labyrinth of dust and dead mice. If it weren't for my decision to sleep on the job that one day, I might never have been confronted about it. If I was never confronted, I would never have claimed to be suicidal. If that hadn't happened, I wouldn't have been committed to the psych ward and I would've had to go back to working at that fucking place.

During the two years I swept and mopped away my dignity, to be a tenant of the Building was the one thing I desired more than anything else. At some point between graduating from college in 2011 and signing the lease to my apartment in 2013, I realized that my childhood had become a cinder at the bottom of an ash can. I had high hopes for 2012, but that year was reduced to smoldering depression like a habit adopted and regretted. 2013 was reminiscent of an atom bomb. The war may have been won, but at what cost?

Despite all I just told you about the Funeral Machine and its evils, the day I moved into the Building was one of the happiest of my life. It symbolized that the years of reality TV shows blaring in the background of my mind were over. One Machine was swapped for another. I was free to make mistakes and not be accountable to Mom and Dad. The Machine is my Daddy now. If I were to trip the Machine's sensors trying to steal myself some kind of freedom, they'd have the Badge slap cuffs on me and drag me to jail. There, I'd learn the true meaning of life. It would be a phrase tattooed on a convict's forearm:

"Live to Think It Twice."

CA-CAW!

"The crows!" Jimmy fell to the floor, clutching his head. "They're gonna kill my mother!" Spittle flew from his mouth in all directions.

"Jimmy, calm down." Dr. Edmund Jeffries, Jimmy's psychiatrist, tried to sound authoritative.

But Jimmy wouldn't calm down. He wailed and thrashed, making his hatred of the avian monstrosities known to the entire building.

"I'll do it!" He wrapped his hands around his own throat. "I'll kill myself if I have to live in a world with *them!*"

It was no use trying to calm him. His mental state had destabilized. Dr. Jeffries dialed for an ambulance to take Jimmy to a psychiatric hospital.

When Jimmy was four years old, a flock of crows attacked him and his mother in the parking lot of a Toys 'R' Us. Three months later, she lost her eye to cancer. Although, to the average person, the two incidents might have seemed unrelated, they were strongly connected in Jimmy's mind. Even now, the sight of a bird — or worse, a crow — would cause the old anxieties to reawaken and gnash their fangs against the bars of his subconscious. These neuroses were the reason he saw Dr. Jeffries for the management of his Zoloft, Zyprexa and Topamax.

Jimmy had dubbed this cocktail the 'ZZ Top regimen.'

Six minutes before the incident in Dr. Jeffries' office, the receptionist called Jimmy's name. Jimmy shut the door gently and seated himself on the pleather chair with the brass buttons. The office was lit with yellow bulbs and smelled of old banana peel.

After closing several windows on his computer, one of them a game of Pong, Dr. Jeffries swung around in his chair and greeted Jimmy with a smile full of coffee stained but otherwise perfectly aligned teeth.

"All right," he said. "If I remember correctly, you are taking..."

"The ZZ Top regimen," Jimmy interjected.

"Oh, right." Dr. Jeffries laughed.

The two made small talk for a few minutes then Dr. Jeffries cleared his throat. "So I understand you're looking to go down on your dosage of Zyprexa because you're concerned about your increased appetite, is that correct?"

Jimmy looked down at his stomach. His once-lean torso had, within two months of taking Zyprexa, become a blubbery mass of hair and stretch marks. "With this gut, I won't be going down on anybody anytime soon." His voice carried no hint of snark.

"That's funny," said Dr. Jeffries, getting the joke. "Okay, sure, so let's help you do that."

He adjusted his glasses. "Now, Jimmy, how would you say your mood has been?"

Jimmy couldn't answer. It was fall: crow season.

The objects of his most primal fears were roosting in

trees and on telephone wires above his house. Flocks of them ate grain on his front lawn and he could hear them from his bedroom. Placid afternoons of video games and net surfing would mutate into anxiety if the volume of his TV and computer weren't turned up all the way. It usually took Jimmy an hour to calm down after a crow encounter. On top of that, he had found out the previous week that his mother's cancer had come out of remission.

Jimmy was convinced that the hole where her eye had been was sending signals to the shadowy imps, telling them where he and his mother were at all times. He could sense them lurking outside her hospital window, perched on branches hidden from view. Whenever he wasn't looking, they'd poke their heads out from behind tree trunks. Their very existence was enough to cause pulsations of paranoia throughout his body. Somewhere on earth, a group of them was plotting to kill him and his family members one by one. He wanted to snap their cocking heads and see them twitch and die in their own blood, but he was too afraid to touch them. The fact that he could never get close enough to kill one was part of the fear. They were too fast. He was afraid to purchase a gun because the crows might just force him to turn it on himself. Even if he killed hundreds, he knew that a thousand more would hatch from eggs gestating in nests of thorns beneath a mocking autumn moon.

"Jimmy, you're zoning out."

Jeffries waved his hand in front of Jimmy's eyes.

Before Jimmy could reply, the one sound he dreaded most in the world found its way through the open window and into his ear drums.

Ca-caw!

After the meltdown in Dr. Jeffries' office, Jimmy was

strapped to a stretcher, loaded into an ambulance, transported to Van Wie Psychiatric Hospital.

He stayed there for a week and a half, but beds were in constant demand and his father's insurance would not cover the full two weeks he needed, so he was discharged early.

Though he was glad to be home, the treatment had been incomplete. All they did was remove one Z and put a T, Thorazine, in its place. He found that this new regimen only muddied his thought processes instead of addressing the actual problem. It made it difficult for him to arrive at any concise emotion besides complacency. His sense of identity had been melon-balled out.

Each day he'd go for long walks, usually ending up at the mall where he'd spend all of his cash on Taco Bell, candy bars and CDs. Boosting his serotonin levels was his only motivator.

Even on the new meds, Jimmy felt dull twinges of nervousness every time he saw a crow. Whenever this happened, he'd perform a mental exercise his counselor at the hospital had taught him. He would focus on the spaces in between thoughts, and picture negative thoughts as boxcars just going on by.

As time went on and the unwanted thoughts became more intrusive, Jimmy found he had to do this exercise often. Thirty days after his discharge, he had to perform it once every other minute. There were just too many crows and other birds pecking, flapping, twitching, and arrogantly cocking their heads. They reminded him of his mother, whose cancer had spread to her brain. His father had broken that news over dinner. Upon hearing it, Jimmy speared his piece of steak with a fork, threw his plate against the wall and stormed upstairs.

Instead of sleeping that night, he ruminated over the empty socket behind his mother's eyepatch: a hole infinitely black, similar to a crow's eye. What kind of consciousness dwelled behind those glassy marbles? How did crows perceive the world around them? What did they think of us if, in fact, they thought at all?

After another couple of weeks, Jimmy began to hate his meds. The dizzy spells when he stood up and the overall blankness of his mood bothered him more than anything. He stopped taking them.

His abstinence from medication lasted only a month. When the police found him ranting and raving about crows in the middle of a city park, he was immediately sent back to Van Wie.

Most days, in between therapy groups, he sat on the floor of his room drawing diagrams of crows with a black marker and labeling each of their organ systems in red. He wanted to understand them. What foul magic made them run? Whose sinister design were they? He had to find out. The stability of his existence depended on it.

He was in the middle of labeling a diagram of a crow's heart when he heard a knock on the door.

"Jimmy?" A staff person named Edwin was at the door. "You have a phone call."

Edwin led Jimmy to a phone booth with a Plexiglas door.

Jimmy flopped into the chair and lifted the receiver.
"Hello?"
"Hi, Jimmy, it's Dad."
"Oh. Hey, Dad. What do you want?"
"Jimmy, it's about your mother."

Jimmy's heart sank. He already knew the outcome of this conversation.

"'The doctors say she's got about a month to live."

He could tell his father was fighting to hold back tears. He could feel his own pouring hot onto his shirt collar.

The crows.

He felt rage climbing the tendons of his neck. He grimaced and clenched his fist. They had gotten his mother, and soon they would come for him. They would not stop until his entire family was dead. They had caused his mother's cancer with the malicious microbes they carried in their beaks. The gene-damaging microbes had made their way through her eye socket and into her brain. Perhaps it was telepathy or nodules unique to the brains of crows which emanated harmful waves causing human cells to reproduce erratically. Jimmy never attempted to pin down exactly what the crows did or intended to do. To him, it was all of the above.

He hung up on his father without a word of goodbye and nodded at Edwin, signaling that he was done using the phone.

Back in his room, he continued to draw, label, outline and sketch, trying to decipher all the patterns and algorithms that constituted the entities to which the English language had attributed the word 'crows.' These were not God's creatures. Not even Satan could cook up such a beast. They had to be the work of Sokar, the whale entity whose purpose was to rend humanity's Creator to the bone and nullify all of existence. He pictured a black cauldron tended by Sokar and his council of mutants. The cauldron was frothing with bubbles, only the bubbles were eggs and the eggs were hatching, releasing a million more squawking abominations into the light of day. He envisioned a crimson sky filled with their black shapes: a backdrop for the blowing of trumpets of Judgment Day. He imagined himself integrated with the bark of a dead oak tree as they tore his face apart with their talons and beaks.

"Bring it on, bitches!" he hollered.

Several staff people's heads turned at once towards his door.

"Bring it ooooooooonnn!"

In a millisecond, Edwin was at the door.

"Jimmy, are you okay in there?" he asked, knocking.

"Yes!" Jimmy laughed. "I'm okay." He dragged himself over to his bed and fished a plastic bag out from between the edge of the mattress and the wall. The bag was filled with dead birds. The birds had manifested from the darkest corner of the ceiling last night and Jimmy had speared them with a pencil. He dumped the birds onto a diagram of the Pentoculon, Sokar's chariot, which he had drawn on hundreds of sheets of loose leaf paper held together by duct tape. The five eyes of the top-like Pentoculon were labeled *mind, soul, heart, wings* and *beak*. He placed a bird carcass on each eye.

"In fact," he reached into his underwear and retrieved a shard of a broken CD, "I'm more than okay." He sliced the palm of his hand and let the blood drip onto each of the dead birds. "I'll never have to fear them again." He grinned. "I've discovered their secrets, Edwin. They can't kill me now. I'm invincible!"

"Jimmy, you're not trying to hurt yourself, are you?"

"No way, man! I'm free from their curse!

I'm unstoppable!" He stepped back, turned around, lowered his head, and with his newfound strength, crashed through the window.

Three staff people including Edwin, burst into the room, but it was too late.

The dead birds on the top diagram startled them, but they quickly noticed that the window had been broken.

Edwin yanked his walkie-talkie out of its holster.

"Brooklodge, this is Edwin over in 4-D. We have an AWOL code red. Repeat, a patient is AWOL. Twenty-one year old Caucasian male, six foot one, brown hair has gone AWOL."

"Copy that. 4-D. We'll set up a perimeter," said the garbled voice on the other end of the walkie.

After fifteen minutes of searching, they finally found Jimmy near the volleyball court. He had stripped naked and was flapping his arms and squawking at groups of crows and other birds. It wasn't long before they converged upon him, restrained him and dragged him back to the unit.

The next day during breakfast, Jimmy felt his mother die. He clutched his chest and fell to the ground, sending a bowl of Rice Krispies flying.

"They've done it!" he howled. "They've killed her!"

Every staff person in the room descended upon Jimmy. One of them radioed for a papoose board.

When the board arrived, Jimmy was strapped to it and carried out of the dining hall. His head writhed and thrashed as he hollered and spat gibberish laced with bird calls and obscenities. The sinews of his neck bulged, and his face was reddish purple.

It wasn't until later that they found out his mother had actually died. His father called minutes after they had injected Jimmy with a PRN and placed him in isolation.

Jimmy was not stable enough to attend the wake or funeral.

Nobody in attendance seemed to notice that two crows, one large and one small, had perched on Jimmy's mother's headstone while the eulogy was read. The birds flew away as soon as they began lowering the casket into the earth. Jimmy's four-year-old cousin Samantha pointed at them with a stubby finger.

"Mama, the big birdies flew away."

"Yes, dear, those were crows."

"Crows. They're ugly. I don't like 'em one bit."

CAVO

The astronauts filed through the airlock, joking with one another about what it would be like to be erased from the universe. Once the airlock had been depressurized, Program Director Charles Winkler punched in the code to open the side hatch. As the hatch slid open, Winkler felt warm endorphins tingling on the back of his neck. His eyes couldn't grow wide enough to take in the panorama of bizarre structures lining the horizon. There were forests of acrylic chrysanthemums, needles sprouting limbs of fiberglass hay, refractive washtub satellite panels, scaffolding decorated with chimes, oceans of chandeliers, and curled ribbons standing still as death. How strange, Winkler thought. CAVO's surface had looked so smooth from Earth.

Six years earlier, a Jupiter-sized gray funnel had appeared in the skies above the planet Alpha Centauri Bb. From the safety of their frigate, a German mining expedition witnessed the obliteration of all matter within the funnel's cone of projection, including the planet. The miners likened the phenomenon to a hologram being switched off.

It wasn't long before another of these objects was discovered halfway between the Moon and Mars. How it had gotten so close without being detected by the thousands of radar dishes all over the globe scanning the cosmos for asteroids and extra-terrestrial messages, no one knew. The scientists of Earth dubbed the object 'CAVO.' The acronym might have stood for 'Catastrophic Astral Vocalization of the Omnipotent' or 'Cataclysmic Amplified Vibrational Oscillator,' but its official title was never finalized.

Although it was determined early on that the situation was hopeless, the governments of Earth agreed that a token effort should be made to quell the threat. Three years after CAVO's discovery, a shuttle carrying four members of the Extra Terrestrial Threat Deterrence Operatives or ETTDO was launched from Kennedy Space Center. Its mission was to investigate and, if possible, destroy the CAVO unit.

Winkler could not keep his heart from fluttering as his toe made contact with the surface. After taking a few steps, he looked down at the ground behind him. His boots had left no footprints, and no one had thought to bring a flag. He glanced back at the crew and they returned his gaze with blank stares.

"All right." Winkler squared his posture like a statue of some famous general. "Shall we begin the investigation?" He scanned the crew decisively.

"Investigation of what?" Star pilot Tanya Clemens slid down the ladder. "Do you seriously believe this thing has some kind of hidden self-destruct button? Does that spiny washcloth sutured to those misshapen ovals look like CAVO's weak spot to you? Is that pipe hidden behind the oblong nerve clock connected to the main reactor? Should we throw a bomb in it? Tell you what: if we find *one* object in this Dadaist funhouse that has any meaning or purpose whatsoever, I'll slit my own oxygen tube."

"Winkler's face reddened. "Yeah, yeah, I get it. We all know this mission is a farce designed to placate the masses. Tell me again about how you three moved so quickly through your stages of grief that nothing in the universe fazes you anymore. Might as well strip naked and start twerking with some quarks in the vacuum of space. Is hope for survival really that much of a buzz kill? My pop-pop wanted to go into space, but he died before he could submit his application. Now I'm living his dream, but nothing is the way it should be. I guess I'll just tag along behind you like a cloud of fart gas and try not to stink up everyone's good time. In the very unlikely case that I did find a way to stop CAVO from going off, would you even care? I'm well aware that it's a statistical impossibility, but an old man's gotta cling on to something."

Computer technician Brad Wilcox plopped down from the ladder. "If ol' Winkle-tits manages to pull the plug on this nonsense machine, I will pay for his hair restoration treatments in full."

Winkler wrung his hands like wounded pigeons. It was all he could do to keep from putting his fist through Brad's helmet and knocking the smirk off of that cocky British face.

The last one out of the airlock was Walter Wiggins, an autistic savant enlisted for his impeccable memory with numbers and fine details. Walter descended each rung gingerly, still humming every Beatles album in order from start to finish as he had been the entire shuttle trip.

After half an hour trudging through a swamp of steel wool, the crew stopped to rest at what looked like a tree with a vertical gash in its side. A cyan orb was imbedded in the gash about a fifth of the way from the top.

"Looks like a vulva and clitoris to me." Brad's breath condensed on the glass of his helmet, obscuring his face. "This place is far out."

Tanya made a face. "By 'far out,' you mean creepy and weird."

"Can't it be both?" Brad put his arm around Tanya's shoulder. "I mean, I can be creepy and weird, but I can be far out too."

Tanya jerked herself away from Brad's grasp with a sound of disgust.

Winkler growled—at Brad, at the situation, he wasn't sure. Probably both.

Brad leaned against a silver celery stalk and slid until his butt hit the ground. "If only there were a pond where we could go skinny dipping."

"There's a pond of spikes over there." Tanya gestured to her right. "Try doing the dead man's float."

"Nah." Brad curled his upper lip like Elvis Presley. "I think I'll save myself for the big ka-boom, thank you very much."

No one laughed. The only sound was Walter's humming.

"Where did Walter go?" said Tanya. "I can hear him, but where did he run off to?"

"He went—" Brad glanced to his right and left. "I dunno. Should we look for him?"

"He's over there," said Winkler, pointing toward a thirteen-foot pane of aqua blue glass jutting out of the ground several yards from their resting place. Walter was behind it. Only the tip of his right glove could be seen.

"Walter, what are you doing over there?" Tanya radioed. "We should stick together in case we need to make a hasty retreat."

The volume of Walter's humming increased.

"Walter, come on, there's a lot more—"

The crew felt a sort of howling: a voice floating on a cold wind calling each of them by name. They exchanged uneasy glances even though they knew wind couldn't travel through space. A second freezing gust stripped away what was left of their morale. Walter began to hum louder and faster. Silence gripped their throats. It seemed as if death lurked within every object and had found a way to whisper incantations directly into their heads:

Unas will beet ewe AUTISTIC width ass teals payed

Sly 'sup you man BEINGS, berry they're buddy sin shall ogre raves

An cough ARE yore chilled wrens phases wit fee seas.

A Lao Sokar too guy dieu threw THE muse sick off CAVO

Two up lace ware pane duh snot egg cyst.

The voice stopped, but the fear remained. The crew was now faced with an ultimatum: let despair pull them under, or shake off their heebie-jeebies and press on with the same black sense of irony that had carried them this far.

"Did you guys hear that?" Winkler tried to smile, but all he could muster was the stretched scowl of a Monday morning office worker. "What a funny way of speaking."

"Yeah," said Brad. "It sounds like an Earth language: perhaps some kind of slang or Creole variation of English."

"It doesn't sound like any language I've ever heard spoken in Trinidad," said Tanya. "But there were two words in that message that stood out to me."

"Unas and Sokar," Walter blurted out suddenly.

Everyone's heads turned toward the aqua blue monolith.

"How did you know?" Tanya's posture stiffened. "That's something my little brother Tim always—"

"His username is ClemDunk10, right?" said Walter.

"Yeah, it is."

"We are members of the same CAVO discussion board on ChurchOfUnas.org." Walter stepped out from behind the monolith. "We've been batting around theories, writing articles and fan-fiction about CAVO ever since it was discovered. One such theory involves two higher-dimensional entities that—"

"Hey, I have an idea," Brad interrupted.

"Let's split up and explore CAVO Scooby-Doo style!"

Walter resumed humming "Maxwell's Silver Hammer."

"How about not?" Winkler snorted.

"We'd be much safer if we traveled in a group."

"Agreed." Tanya folded her arms.

"Okay, okay, sheesh." Brad rolled his eyes.

"I was only joking."

Walter nodded in acquiescence.

After trekking two miles through a forest of ashy pine cones adorned with aquamarine jewels, the crew felt CAVO begin to vibrate. The vibrations loosened hundreds of cones from their branches, sending them clattering to the ground.

"Look out!" Brad threw a stray cone at Tanya and it bounced off her shoulder.

"Very funny." Her expression was stern despite Brad's smirking and giggling.

"Yeah, I agree." Brad plucked another cone from one of the larger cones. "A lot funnier than this rumbling we're experiencing. Should we even venture a guess as to what's causing it?"

"I dunno. It depends on whether it would be fun or

interesting to do so. What do you think? You're the computer technician after all."

Brad leaned against a large tree. "Hmm, perhaps we should commence a discourse of philosophical inquiry. Computer science was not my first love, you know. That honor belongs to none other than philosophy."

"Okay, Mr. Philosopher. Let's do some philosophizing. But first, we should probably get out of this forest. I don't like the looks of the dangly blue tampon things hanging from those pine cones."

"Blue tampon things?" Brad couldn't help but laugh. "I wonder what kind of creature ... oops, never mind, ew, bad thoughts."

Tanya laughed. Brad was convinced this was the first time she'd ever done so.

As if on cue, the vibrations stopped.

Once out of the pine cone forest, the crew made camp near the edge of a canyon filled with jade bubbles and twisted pieces of metal.

"Tanya?" Brad reclined against a segmented hollow log-worm. "What do you think CAVO is?"

Tanya grunted. "From what I've seen, I think it's whatever will fuck with the human mind the most."

"I agree." Brad gazed up at the stars, imagining CAVO units stationed near each of their planets, poised to eradicate them. The thought disturbed him, so he chased it out of his mind. "I can't help but think that there's got to be some rhyme or reason to all these formations. I mean, look at those metal things in that canyon over there. Is it just me, or do they look an awful lot like rhino heads, or even triceratops?"

"But they're not." Tanya adjusted herself. "It's the same as looking at clouds or ink blot tests back on Earth. Their shapes are arbitrary; we only see what we project onto them.

In a sense, they become whatever we want them to be. Their only consistent attribute is their strangeness as seen from our point of view. It's almost as if they were made to be misunderstood. Same goes for CAVO as a whole. Remember how it showed up in our solar system without being detected? And what about its method of destroying planets? Totally unexplainable. I feel like it exists for the sole purpose of fucking with us."

"Here's a thought." Brad held up a finger. "What if the mind fuck didn't begin with CAVO? What if the existence of mankind was just one massive hallucination?"

"My brother used to prattle on about stuff like that all the time." Tanya smiled once more. Her smile made Brad blush. "Once CAVO extinguishes Polaris and Betelgeuse, it will be as if we never existed. We never made contact with aliens, so there will be no one to remember us. We will vanish without a trace, and the universe will be no better or worse for it."

"Yep," Brad nodded. "We'll just be turned off like an image on a TV screen. Maybe that's all we ever were: just a matrix of dots depicting something real, the fate of which can be decided by the simple twist of a knob ... *boop!* ... TV time's over. Time to eat dinner with the family. No more universe."

Tanya laughed again.

To Brad, it sounded like the tinkling of Christmas bells.

The crew had made it two miles past the canyon when Walter began to point excitedly at a waist-high mesa studded with three turquoise jewels arranged in an equilateral triangle. The others agreed to stop and check it out as well.

"Make sure you stay hydrated," said Winkler to the others.

Walter kept himself from becoming over stimulated by humming "Lucy in the Sky with Diamonds."

"I wonder what this triangular formation is." Winkler pointed a gloved finger at the mesa.

"Nothing here makes sense," said Brad. "Might as well be an abstract art museum."

Walter hummed the second verse of "Lucy" while pretending to gaze out beyond the mesa at a city of crystal obelisks. In reality, he was eavesdropping on Winkler and Brad.

"You know," said Winkler, "I'm honestly as disconnected from this whole thing as you and Tanya."

Walter recalled that the middle-aged program director had been the only one to ever take the mission seriously. All throughout training, the crew had done nothing but play Texas Hold 'Em and foosball, smoke hand-rolled cigarettes, and watch reruns of South Park. Walter didn't participate in cards, but kept everyone entertained by performing Beethoven's piano sonatas on a digital keyboard.

For the first few days, Winkler tried to redirect the crew's focus toward the mission, but no one besides Walter ever seemed motivated to get up earlier than noon. Winkler would hold meetings and Walter would show up only to hear Brad quote sayings from a book titled *The Wisdom of the Great Philosopher Testicles* (pronounced, of course, to rhyme with Sophocles.) After a week of trying and failing miserably to rally his audience, Winkler stopped holding meetings.

On his daily trip to the vending machine to purchase his lunchtime can of Sprite, Walter would always find Winkler sitting alone in the hall, drinking scotch and club soda. The two would meet eyes for a second before resuming their broken cuckoo clock routines.

"At first, I wanted to make a difference," said Winkler. "I sincerely believed that the human race could stop CAVO.

But now that I've had some time to think about it—" He gestured toward the Earth. Since the widespread implementation of Smart Pathogens, the planet had taken on the hue of dirty bathwater. Over the course of eons, it had germinated, ripened, and was now rotting both inside and out. What remained was the corpse of a world: a dead, utilitarian orb choked by the varicose veins of post-capitalist oligarchies.

"—I get the feeling that humanity's end has arrived, and maybe it's about time. Human existence is nothing but a joke without a punchline. Or rather, the punchline is that everyone dies; which isn't really a punchline because it isn't funny. Such a joke serves no purpose because it is illogical. Perhaps *life itself* is illogical. The only way to compensate for the failed joke known as life is to pass your immortal genes onto the next generation so that perhaps your future incarnations might not make the same mistakes as you and your ancestors."

Walter saw that Brad's eyes were not focused on Winkler, but rather a structure above their heads resembling a pair of breasts with thirteen nipples pierced with safety pins supporting bridges made of lozenges and crab claws.

"And besides," Winkler continued, "what would become of us even if we did find a way to halt our destruction? How many more centuries could we survive on that dung ball anyway? God bless the people rich enough to emigrate to Betelgeuse or Polaris. Hopefully, CAVO doesn't discover those worlds anytime soon."

Winkler let out a sigh that vibrated his lips.

"Who am I kidding? Even if the Polarians and Betelgeusians started scanning for habitable planets and building emigration vessels three years ago, it would still be too late if a CAVO unit were to appear in their midst today. There's no doubt in my mind that who or whatever is behind CAVO will succeed in blotting out humanity. This is it. We're done."

Winkler shook his head and emitted a laugh that didn't seem quite real.

"All that remains now is to have a drink, laugh at the futility of our efforts, and wait for the guillotine blade to fall. God damn, I wish I'd filled my tank with gin instead of water. It would've been nice to stare death in the face amped up on Beefeater rather than being fully aware of what an old sack of shit I've become. Oh well. Hey Brad, you wanna hear a joke?"

Before Winkler could tell his joke, the ground began to rumble.

A sphere of aqua-blue matter bubbled up beneath Walter and wrapped a feeler around his ankle. He knew that if it penetrated his suit and made contact with his skin, it would hijack his central nervous system and detach his mind from reality. This was a phenomenon he and Tim Clemens had read about in arcane texts such as *The Gospel of Unas* and *The Sokarian Manuscripts*. These tomes of the Unasian and Sokarian religious cults described the inner workings of the CAVO units as well as the universe. They had predicted CAVO's arrival, but so far, no one had found a way to prevent the units from destroying their targets.

"Rocking horse people eating marshmallow pies ..."

"Geez, Walter, settle down, you're giving me a headache."

Walter hoped that by humming an orderly and well-structured song, he could dislodge this little tendril of chaos from his leg.

"The song is supposed to fade out Walter. Why are you continuing to—"

The mesa began to pull itself apart. Walter fell in first. The feeler, still wrapped around his ankle, assimilated with a pool of iridescent blue liquid at the bottom of the pit and continued to drag him down. He grasped Tanya's leg. Thankfully, Tanya had thought to bear-hug Winkler's torso. Walter dug his free boot into the side of the chasm for leverage.

"Grab my hand!" Brad offered a meaty arm to Winkler.

Winkler grasped it, and Tanya shrieked when Winkler began to slip.

Walter hummed as loudly and passionately as he could. The hairs on the back of his neck stood up in appreciation for the Fab Four: his favorite band since he was four years old. He remembered watching reruns of the Beatles' Ed Sullivan performances on a channel devoted to vintage television. He thought of John and Yoko standing naked in their living room. How liberating it must've been to not give a fuck and embrace love, peace and music like a flower-haired girl swinging on a tire in the summer rain. Someday, perhaps soon, Walter would reach the doorstep of serenity. He imagined himself knocking three times on the door, and a shimmering hand inviting him in. Beyond the realm of physicality, there would be no social cues to misinterpret: just infinite light and acceptance.

As if the steady rhythm section of George and Ringo had given him the boost he needed, Walter kicked off with his foot, allowing Brad to get a good enough grasp on Winkler's wrist to lift the three of them out of the pit.

Once the astronauts regained their bearings, they made their way to the edge of the fissure and peered down into it. Walter was surprised that the aqua blue liquid wasn't rising up to attack them. Winkler was about to speak, but hushed when Tanya indicated that something was moving beneath the liquid's surface. Walter stiffened for a second, but relaxed when he saw that it was only a flat, black rectangle supported by a pole.

"So, there *are* moving parts on this thing," said Winkler.

A rod of blue light extended from the rectangle's center and widened, forming a holographic screen.

The four astronauts waited for something else to happen, but nothing did. As soon as they were confident that the risk had lessened, they crept closer to marvel at the screen.

"Looks like a computer monitor, doesn't it?" said Winkler.

"I wouldn't touch it," said Tanya. "We don't know enough about it."

"Oh, come on!" Winkler sneered. "Where's your sense of adventure? We know we're all very likely to die here anyway. This thing might contain invaluable information about CAVO: maps, blueprints, schematics. I daresay we might even find a way to shut the damn thing down and save mankind!"

Tanya's skepticism was clear on her face.

"The only way to find out what it does is to examine it scientifically." Winkler adjusted his suit sleeves. "I'm gonna go over there and discern for myself just what in the hell it is."

As if in anticipation of Winkler, a bridge extended from the ravine's edge to the pedestal. He ambled across it. When he was close enough, he touched it with his index finger. The screen sprang to life.

Walter, still humming, bounded across the bridge and stood next to Winkler.

Winkler seemed mesmerized by the images flashing before his eyes.

Walter trained his focus not on the images themselves, but their reflections in Winkler's glasses.

The screen showed spliced footage of baby doll heads with hollowed-out eyes, cables plugged into outlets painted white, Christmas ornaments falling from hemlock branches, a pope-like figure waving to a crowd of millions, a glass of spoiled milk, a razor blade, a bullet tearing through a hard-boiled egg, stock footage of Adolf Hitler superimposed over a 1980's exercise video, and finally, a string of the following characters:

cabRETROʧʞg alfic, nee⚲ne si4frʒic cataphone VIRUS supemarket ac⊑pha8gm. Pe╪cturʁkeecia, confla7ages ig≠IFscan recЦn CAVOral rezin for scene and science for ATTEMPTSder c5acntal ؎ or6gʤ idealistic udo 4x■ co↔lke reazi ... 01TO10 ... 7dhs Pʄero7ȸ\, {]] ῶion crush-SCRAMBLE ... n2g ... ∑explclmag b‿tANus8 ... c⊕ien∹⊐‡e ... 2 ... I was ˠ⊢nce a hɷro AUTISTIC niД̲ma sti®t2 w@ ... enMINDdy ogጠve been, sce44♫8zoo ... dmf4yl' ITage ... this is the WILL ... ooc711sgشщ, RESULT oř cle ... 414end q30 IN o§astioss ... peCAVOne ... BECOMIN-Ga⌂m ῶer ... Ʊ13sparg8> It's depicting the noise of the autistic mi1UNSCRAMBLED ?9xﷺא do№ **8d4g! ...

The screen began to swirl with colors, patterns, shapes, diagrams of slave ships labeled with the year 1621, fountains oozing translucent goo, and an old man's testicles being crushed in a trash compactor.

"Enjoying yourselves over there guys?"

Tanya's voice crackled through the radio.

Walter was entranced.

"Winkler, what's your status?"

Walter noticed that Winkler had stopped moving, but was too engrossed in the reflected images to heed anything going on around him.

Winkler gave no answer.

"Winkler, do you copy?"

Nothing.

Tanya dashed across the bridge with Brad in tow. When they reached the spot where Winkler stood motionless, Tanya tapped his shoulder. "Winkler, you okay?" She grasped and shook him. He collapsed into her arms, face expressionless, a rope of drool dangling from his slack lower lip, tear ducts bleeding.

"Walter!" Tanya nearly shouted into her comm. device. "What happened to Winkler?"

"Nothing," Walter wanted to say, but that was not accurate. What had happened to Winkler was something that not even the most gifted expert at neurotypical communication could explain. In the most basic terms available, *the opposite of nothing* had happened to Winkler. Walter, with the right and left hemispheres of his brain fused in a crucial location that rendered him unable to tie his shoes but gave him the ability to understand the cosmos and our place in it, hummed the last line of "Lucy" and stopped.

"I will tell you what happened to Winkler," he said, "but in order to do that, I need to first elaborate on the nature of CAVO. Only then will you understand."

"Are you shitting me right now, Walter?" Brad's brows furrowed. "Just tell us what the hell happened to—"

"Easy now." Tanya grabbed Brad's arm. She looked directly into Walter's eyes. "We don't have time to speculate about CAVO. Winkler needs medical attention. We need to bring him back to the ship."

"The man you knew as Winkler is dead." Walter nudged Winkler's limp body with his foot, causing it to flop about like a Halloween decoration. "His mind has become completely compromised. I suppose you could say he is now in a permanent catatonic state. Whether we drag him along or leave him here makes no difference. He is no longer connected with reality. But in a sense, neither are we."

Tanya and Brad looked at each other.

"What do you mean?" Tanya raised a discerning eyebrow.

"We severed our ties to ordinary perception the moment we set foot on CAVO's surface." Walter gently arranged Winkler's body in a stable position. "CAVO will shatter every preconceived notion we had about the universe, and then we ourselves will be destroyed. But, if we choose to adjust our point of view, we can interpret this loss of structure as a new type of freedom. Our lives have become a stream-of-consciousness poem or an abstract piece of art. We are no longer bound by the restrictions of a world that has to make sense. We can do anything and be anything!"

Walter put an arm around both Brad and Tanya's shoulders and led them back across the bridge, leaving Winkler propped against the pedestal like a bum passed out in an alley.

Tanya looked over her shoulder at Winkler's inert figure. "Should we...go back for him? I could swear he was waving..."

"No," said Walter. "We need to move on. I'm not certain, but I think CAVO is trying to tell me something. We need to keep exploring in order to find out what it is."

"Do we now?" Tanya glanced sidelong at Brad.

"Yes," said Walter. "It will take some time for my brain to process this information, so for now, let's just put the imminent threat of CAVO out of our minds and wander this land of nonsense and see what we can discover!"

"Whatever you say, mate." Brad grinned.

Tanya eyed Brad coldly.

At first, Tanya and Brad felt iffy about leaving Winkler. But the more they wandered around with Walter, taking in sight after strange and inexplicable sight, the more they realized that normal human reactions to stimuli such as emotions and

logical connections were being eroded by the chaotic weird-
ness of CAVO.

And perhaps that wasn't such a bad thing.

Eventually, Tanya's posture relaxed and she became
unable to stop smiling. At some point, Brad jettisoned all his
negative emotions and felt his heart expand and soften like a
marshmallow in a microwave. The vibrations started up
once again. Glancing around them, the remaining crew
members noticed the needles of the cacti vibrating like dirty
tuning forks.

At the bottom of a valley flanked by metal rings ridged with
medicine bottles and fractal feathers, the crew happened
upon a cluster of rectangular prisms vaguely resembling a
city. They climbed the "stairs" of one of these "buildings,"
pushed aside some debris and were delighted to find an
enclosed structure reminiscent of a "room."

Tanya and Brad sat down together on a slab of collapsed
drywall. Walter examined a bluish glass plate embedded in
the wall while humming "A Day in the Life."

The vibrations increased in intensity, causing a piece of
ceiling to crash down right next to them. Brad jumped and
Tanya gasped. Walter took no notice.

"Is something up with Walter? What's he doing over
there?"

"It looks like he found something."

Tanya and Brad shuffled over to where Walter was
gazing slack-jawed at a round piece of glass that might have
been a stained-glass window or mandala. Its pattern was like
a star-shape with an ever-shifting number of points. At the
end of each point were symbols, characters, words and
numerals both alien and familiar.

"What is this thing?" Tanya ran her fingers over the
glass. "What does this all mean?"

Brad craned his head to get a better look. "I don't get it. It seems completely random to me." He attempted to read the symbols and words aloud. "1D, ⱧI, Severity, tweΨCgl, 88I8, orgumP, 7Lx7, (+E oS▦ng⊣ <eaOlϹl, F, something that looks like a baby scribbled it with a crayon, 8ⱰbB, ꓴ?E ^‡T, Ha⌐i₤, >%L, ΛE **FAX**, MΛb₹d, more incomprehensible gibberish. Who or whatever came up with this was either on meth or having a manic episode."

Tanya rolled her eyes. "Well put, Brad. But out of all the formations we've seen, I feel like this is the only one aside from the big blue screen of death that has some kind of meaning behind it. Perhaps we can trace some of these points to one another, you know, see what connects to what."

"Okay, here goes." Brad placed his finger on the symbol "Ы" and traced it down and across the mandala to where it met the word "o3nhc∞."

"See?" he folded his arms. "Nothing but gobbledy-gook."

"Let me try." Tanya placed her finger on "o.o] □ ⌁[," and traced the line connecting it to "Taꞑˠ₳Ϲ|ₐᵐƏN5ɰı| ∟Δ13."

"Tanya Clemens will die?" A fluttery laugh escaped her throat. "What the fuck? That can't be what it says."

"Really? Let me see." Brad narrowed his eyes, scrutinizing the spot where Tanya's finger rested. "Tan... ya... Cle... mens... will..." Brad looked at Tanya. "Yup, that's what it says. It's not exactly the Queen's English, but given what the letters look like they spell, I'm pretty sure that's the message it's trying to send."

"But that makes no sense." Tanya shook her head. "How did CAVO know who I was and that I would come here?"

Brad cracked his neck. "Maybe Walter's right. Maybe there are things about this universe our brains are just too small to understand. Maybe you, I, and everybody else have been under the surveillance of a higher presence since the beginning of time. You might call it 'God,' but I prefer to call it Crocodile Dundee, Man of the Wilderness, immune to shark bites and all other forms of natural carnage."

"Idiot," Tanya mumbled under her breath. "But seriously, how does it know about me and my future? Why does it think I'm going to die?"

"Aren't we all going to die here? Look at Winkler." Brad gestured vaguely back to where they'd left him. "This is CAVO, remember? The ominous alien speaker from the nether realm poised to blast human existence into oblivion with its evil sound waves." Brad wiggled his fingers like he was telling a scary story around a campfire.

Tanya grimaced.

The terrain began to vibrate much more intensely than before.

Walter had finished humming the entirety of "Sgt. Pepper" and was now on "The White Album."

"Do you think she's gonna blow soon?"

"Your guess is as good as mine." Brad clonked his helmet against Tanya's in a friendly gesture.

Walter's arm snapped upright: his finger pointing directly at the mandala.

From the corners of their eyes, Tanya and Brad watched the mandala recede into the wall and slide to the right, revealing a blue tunnel. They stumbled backwards.

"I think we'd better get out of here." Brad began to glance every which way.

"Yeah." Tanya reflexively grabbed Brad's arm. "I'd say we've been given a fair warning. Who knows what might come out of that thing."

The three of them scrambled over the heap of collapsed ceiling and searched for the door through which they had entered.

"There's too much debris." Brad attempted to lift a chunk of ceiling and failed. "It's too dark. I can't see where we came in."

"Over there!" Tanya pointed at a doorframe blocked by several twisted girders. "Looks like a lot of shrapnel to climb over, but I think we can make it."

An incessant buzz like a fire alarm began to sound, making the three of them jump.

"What the hell is that sound?" Brad cocked his head toward the tunnel where the mandala had been."

"Whatever it is, it's obnoxious." Tanya shouted.

Walter's hands were plastered to the sides of his helmet, his body gyrating as if he was in severe pain.

"It's like someone's dumped a swarm of bees into my helmet." Brad began to tear at clods of powdery infrastructure blocking the way to the exit. "We'd better move fast."

The buzzing combined with the increasing vibrations of CAVO created an effect which, to the astronauts, felt like their brains were being fucked with barbed stingers.

"I think it's coming from that tunnel." Brad's vocal cords were starting to shred.

"What?"

"I said... Never mind, hold on."

"What!"

"I'll be right back!" Brad broke away from Tanya and began to climb back over the rubble heap toward the hole. If he could plug it up with something, maybe the noise would stop.

Amongst the rubble, he found a rock that looked large enough to at least muffle the god-awful drone. Even in gravity less than Earth's, the rock was incredibly heavy. He tried fashioning a lever and fulcrum out of a triangular piece of rock and a girder, but it was no use.

"Walter!" Brad shouted, hoping he could hear him. "Help me lift this rock!"

Walter removed his hands from his ears, hobbled over to Brad, bent down and thrust his hands beneath the rock.

"On three, we lift. Ready? One ... two ..."

They were just barely able to drag the rock across the room and hoist it into the hole. The rock was in, but the sound still blared. They needed to seal it with something.

"Walter, I need your eye for detail. Find something to caulk this hole."

Walter sauntered off toward a section of the room neither of them had explored.

Meanwhile, Brad kept his eyes peeled for Tanya. She must still be on the other side of the debris pile. Shit. If only we could hear each other. We've gotta seal that hole quick.

By an uncanny stroke of luck, Walter discovered what appeared to be a drainpipe oozing sticky black material. This would have to do. He scooped up as much of the viscous substance as he could, carried it in handfuls across the room, and mashed it into the spaces unsealed by the rock.

After what felt like hours, he was finally able to seal off the blue tunnel and dull the raucous buzzing. Brad and Walter's ears rang like they had been blasted with feedback from walls of Marshall amplifiers.

"Tanya?" Brad called out, not sure if he was saying anything at all. This must be what it's like to be deaf, he thought: having to rely on the vibrations of your vocal cords to ascertain that you're making sound.

"Tanya?" He and Walter scoured the whole room: the debris pile, the area surrounding the drainpipe and another corner they had neglected to explore. There was still no sign of the Trinidadian. Perhaps she had found a way out.

As they walked past the entrance for the third time, Walter noted that the girders had been pushed aside enough to for a person to slip through. Ah ha! Brad smirked. *She's probably waiting for us outside, unable to hear a thing.*

Brad and Walter clambered over the pieces of wall, pipes, and sword-like protrusions. As they descended the stairs, Brad noticed something unusual. It was a white tube, apparently severed by a piece of metal jutting out of the wall. As they got closer, a sensation of a cold lead orb formed in Brad's chest and dropped through his guts. *Wait a minute,* he thought, *this looks like...*

As they turned the corner, Brad's eyes traced the tube to a space suit: Tanya's. She lay motionless on the steps, sprawled out on her back, dead. Her oxygen tube had gotten snagged on that piece of metal. She had fallen. It had been an accident.

Brad looked at Walter and tried to speak even though he couldn't hear. The only stimuli his brain could acknowledge were the vibrations. Their intensity and frequency were increasing with each passing minute. Brad watched solemnly as Tanya's white, oxygen-starved eyes rattled along to the funeral dirge CAVO had composed just for the human race.

Walter and Brad stepped out into the eternal night of CAVO. For perhaps the first time in his adult life, Brad found himself fighting the urge to cry.

He and Walter sat on an enclosure surrounding a smooth blue lump with blue marbles frozen inside of it.

"Walter?" Brad croaked after finally winding himself up enough to speak at all. "What does this all mean?"

Walter's eyes betrayed no emotion save for the occasional twitch of one of his under-eye bags.

"You're probably going to be the last person I ever talk to." A tear ran down Brad's cheek. "And just so you know, I'm honored. You're a really articulate and brilliant guy. You

save your words for when they really count, and I respect
that."

Walter didn't smile, but he nodded slowly in Brad's
direction.

"By some miracle," Brad continued, "I get to spend my
final moments with someone who probably knows more
about CAVO than anyone else. I don't know how you
obtained this information. You could be pissing in the wind
for all I know. If there's one thing I know for sure, it's that I
don't wanna leave this world without answers. Even if
they're just tall tales, please tell me everything."

Walter's gaze seemed to have connected itself to a star
on the horizon.

Brad recognized the star as the middle of Orion's belt.

"If you're sure you want to know," said Walter, "I'll start
at the beginning."

To Brad, it seemed as though the starlight, laced with
wisdom and knowledge, was being poured into Walter's
mind.

"I'm sure." Brad hung his head like a condemned man
making peace with the world before the opening of the
gallows trapdoor.

Walter cleared his throat. "The CAVO units are lower-
dimensional extensions of an entity called Sokar who often
takes the form of a sperm whale. Sokar represents dark
energy, entropy, the destructive force that leads the universe
to its ultimate end. He is the Yin aspect of the Yin/Yang
duality that governs our universe; Yang being the colossal
squid Unas, the creative force, the will to overcome entropy.
Unas creates countless temporary universes (ours being one
of them) from which he harvests and consumes the spirits of
deceased intelligent organisms that have evolved within
them. These spirits provide Unas with the nourishment he
needs to defend against Sokar who seeks to destroy him and,
by extension, our universe.

"The universes Unas makes can be likened to fruit. Whenever a new universe germinates, undercover Sokarian agents inject billions of CAVO units into them. These units are essentially viruses designed to cut off Unas's food supply by either erasing or stupefying sentient races.

"CAVO units can assume any shape. In some cases, they disguise themselves as planets and stars. This is alarming considering that Earth and planets like it may have been CAVO units all along. The totality of life in the universe may just be one big hallucination induced by CAVO. Then again, this line of thinking could easily be the result of CAVO's influence on my thought process. All we can know for sure is that CAVO units tailor their appearance and behavior to fit the schema of whatever is most befuddling to their observers.

"This unit we're standing on elucidates my point perfectly. It destroys matter with sound waves even though we know that

A.) sound cannot travel through space, and

B.) matter cannot be destroyed.

This leads to confusion on our part when we try to comprehend it. CAVO weakens our grounding in reality by openly defying its laws. It achieves this with a weapon called the Confusion Wave. This Wave alters the subjective reality of anyone in its vicinity. The odd formations dotting CAVO's surface, the images and words displayed on its screens as well as its method of destroying planets are all phantasms crafted specifically to fry our logic centers.

"When a person's mind is bombarded by stimuli it can't comprehend, the person becomes 'unglued,' so to speak. They start to exhibit symptoms of schizophrenia or mania. The confusion overwhelms them and they shut down due to their inability to make sense of reality."

"So that's what happened to Winkler." Brad nodded.

"Precisely." Walter adjusted his helmet. "And CAVO's

prediction of Tanya's death is another example of its ability to alter any given observer's subjective reality. The 'real' Tanya may be alive in a pocket universe somewhere whereas the 'deceased' Tanya is a hallucination we both share. If a third party were to enter the picture, they'd probably end up joining in on said hallucination.

"Far out." Brad cracked his knuckles.

Walter's eyes lit up. "You want to know something really far out?" He flashed Brad a toothy grin. "For the last couple of hours, my subconscious has been piecing together fragments of information broadcasted from an outside source and channeled through CAVO's informational static. It took awhile, but now I'm certain of the message's contents. As it turns out, there *is* a way to stop CAVO."

"Are you fucking serious?" Brad sprung upright. "Then, come on; let's blow the bloody thing to Hell!"

Walter held up a hand and Brad reseated himself.

"The message is somewhat vague, but from what I understand of it, CAVO's weakness is something called the CAVO Retro Virus. It is exactly what it sounds like: an antidote to the CAVO virus."

"How do we get a hold of this Retro Virus?" The lines in Brad's forehead betrayed his apprehension.

Walter's eyes met Brad's. "I *am* the CAVO Retro Virus." He looked down at his feet. "All autistic people are. I'm not sure why, but the message was clear about what I have to do."

"What do you mean?" Brad swallowed. "Don't tell me you're gonna sacrifice yourself."

Walter's adam's apple moved down and up his throat like a mouse under a blanket. "I need to let CAVO try and scramble my mind. If all goes well, the Confusion Wave will backfire, causing CAVO to unscramble itself. For reasons I can't explain, autistic minds deflect mental scramblers. This will thrust CAVO into the realm of physicality and render its planet-destroying mechanism useless. We need to find one of those computer screens quick before CAVO enacts defensive—"

Walter had barely gotten the words out when familiar javelins of cold fear speared them from below.

"Fuck!" Walter screamed. "We're too late."

The cold snaked up their intestines, froze their stomachs and climbed their esophagi. The voice they had heard at the beginning of their journey began to speak once again:

You're whirled is gnome oar.

Walter scanned his surroundings for Brad. He found him impaled on an aqua blue javelin several feet away. His face was gray and his eyes were rolled back, revealing purplish veins.

Walter felt despair working its way through his body. He wanted so badly to give up and let CAVO have him. But then he remembered. At this very moment, CAVO was trying to scramble him. All he had to do was resist: exercise the indomitable will of a man whose brain doesn't run concurrent with the rest of the world, a man long frustrated with neurotypical definitions of "sense" and "nonsense."

"That's not true!" Walter hollered. "The world will continue even after we're all gone."

Snuff doubt buy freak when sees mortar riff-eyeing then yard-adds creaming 'ah-choo!'

Walter thought about his father and how, growing up, he never understood why young Walter would overreact to even the tiniest of annoyances. He needed to forgive his father. The man had tried his best despite the mistakes he made.

He was human after all.

"I've overcome that fear," Walter spat. "I'll never let fear of punishment control me ever again!"

Hiss Mao though pens why dearth an Hume an fizzy Allah Jeep perm hits, Cree eight ting annoys lichen Ann grease warm-off whore-nets chaise sing Anne awe tit stick id inn too ah fern ace.

"Loud sounds do bother me," Walter admitted. "But as long as I can stim and practice mindfulness, I will endure them."

Butt dune hot diss pair: twill bee oh Furby furlong.

"Not if I have anything to say about it!"

The javelin retreated back into the ground, leaving Walter on his hands and knees, gasping for breath.

When he was finally able to rise to his feet, he saw something he could never have been prepared for. It was a statue of a man impaled on a javelin. The statue was made of umbrella handles, porcelain spiders, gears and misshapen marbles. It appeared to be wearing Brad's glasses. Or were they a pair of glass mushrooms threaded together with frozen caterpillars?

It didn't work. Walter felt his soul sink through his feet. *Goddamn it all! Maybe I'm just not autistic enough. Who knew there'd come a time when not being autistic enough would prevent you from saving the world. Oh fucking well.* He hung his head. *I suppose I have two choices at this point: either wait for CAVO to obliterate humanity, or strip naked and start twerking with some quarks in the vacuum of space.*

Walter pictured quarks dancing everywhere like bacteria in a petri dish. The formations around him started to move. *What the hell?* He tried to stop imagining it, but everything continued to wiggle as if the edges of reality had become a Dr. Katz cartoon. The statue's glasses were now actual glass mushrooms held together by live caterpillars. Each of their little legs moved like true-to-life butterfly larvae. It seemed like every object was becoming the thing which before it had only vaguely resembled. The Rubik's cubes made of slide whistles became Rubik's cubes and slide whistles precariously held together. The half-bells began to grow actual mirrored tilt-a-whirls, and the combs grafted to the doorknobs suspended above lakes of frozen moons became exactly what Walter had envisioned them as. CAVO and all its formations were becoming tangible and concrete.

Had he done it? Had the Confusion Wave reversal worked after all? *Yes*, he thought. The plan had succeeded, but the victory was bittersweet. It was too late for Brad and the others. By the time the deflected Confusion Wave had brought coherency to CAVO, the bodies and souls of Walter's crewmates had already become integrated with it. The only thing left for him to do was signal for a ride home and inform the military of his mission's success.

We need to send astronauts with autism to every CAVO unit mankind discovers. He pressed a button on the smartphone grafted to his suit's left sleeve. *We have our trump card now. The future of humanity rests in the hands of those on the spectrum.*

"Mission control, this is Walter Wiggins. The CAVO unit has been neutralized, repeat, the CAVO unit has been neutralized. Requesting an evac ship, over."

The minutes following Walter's communication with Mission Control passed like sap through the trunk of a pine. His leg began to shake uncontrollably. *What if CAVO is still operational, but I just don't know it? What if everything that just happened is yet another mind fuck?* He glanced around

him. A miniature dump truck with a bird's beak was
splashing about in a bird bath grafted to a horse with hooves
made of silicon spaghetti.

*Even if that's true, I need to make peace with fate. In at
least one reality, I figured out how to defeat CAVO and save
mankind. If, by some cruel twist, CAVO wins in the end, at
least I can say I went down swinging.*

"Copy that, Walter," said a woman's voice. "Congratulations on a successful mission. You've done a great thing for
humanity. ETA for the evac ship is 1400 hours. Stand by in
the shuttle until then. Over and out."

Relief poured over Walter like butter on pancakes.
Reality is back to normal, he sighed. *Thanks to me.* He felt a
twinge of dread at the prospect of walking back to the ship,
but quickly reminded himself that a long walk was the least
of his worries.

I guess I'd better get a move on. He booted up his smartphone's GPS. The ship appeared as a blinking beacon on
the screen. *Twenty-two miles, huh? That's almost a
marathon.*

As he walked, he thought about his parents, siblings, and
most of all, his online buddy, Tim Clemens.

*I should buy a plane ticket and fly to Trinidad as soon as
I can scrounge up the money. Tim is gonna need all the
support he can get after the government breaks the news to
him. Maybe we can go to a LARPing event when I get there.
We won't do a sci-fi campaign though; that would be in poor
taste. Medieval fantasy sounds like the way to go.*

Walter glanced over his shoulder for one last look at
CAVO's landscape. He saw various objects here and there
that he recognized, but nothing to write home about. After
that, he resolved to only look forward.

A FREE RIDE TO PLEROMA

While exploring the woods behind her house, Bobbie-Sue Viola came upon a strange tree. Its branches spiraled and twisted like sea worms. Unfamiliar symbols were carved into its trunk. "Maybe aliens visited here and planted seeds they brought with them." She ran her fingers over the symbols until she felt a sharp pain. "Ow!" She pulled her hand back. Could the tree be poisonous? She wiped her fingers with the hem of her hoodie sleeve. "Nah," It was probably just a cramp from all the graph homework Mrs. Mallory had assigned. And the alien writing was most likely neighborhood kids doing graffiti.

A gurgle rose from her stomach. It was getting close to dinner time. "Goodbye, tree. I'll try and figure you out later." She scampered toward the forest entrance using the green mesh of the fence as a beacon to find her way home.

The Quantum Prison confining the witch Mirtha was located within the atomic latticework of a glass sunflower belonging to a twenty-something-year-old studying graphic design at Sage College in Albany, New York. Mirtha had been trapped there by the brave knight Ralphus after he had foiled her attempt to shift the earth's magnetic field and destroy mankind.

Sitting cross legged on the floor of her hovel, Mirtha glided her finger over the surface of the Mirror-Window or 'Mirrow.' She had come across the door-sized Mirrow several years ago while searching the endless corridors of the Prison for a means of escape. It had stood glistening amongst a pile of debris amassed by glassants who used the refuse as building materials for their hills.

Mirtha dragged the Mirrow back to her hovel, leaned it against the wall, sat down and gazed into it. It showed her every possible manifestation of reality at once, triggering a Revelation in her brain: reality was essentially a dualistic system. There was the Inside (a.k.a. the Labyrinth or Multiverse where humans and other creatures lived), and the Outside, which was a solid, infinite whole. The Outside was a place without sound, color, waves, particles, or any sort of division between objects in space/time. After studying her reflection, as well as the reflections of reflections within her reflection, her life's goal became clear. As soon as she escaped from the Prison, she'd bust down a fire door and bask in the freedom of the Outside.

The image currently displayed in the Mirrow was a young girl named Bobbie-Sue Viola. The girl had stumbled upon a Conduit Tree (one of which existed in every possible reality), which the Mirrow used as inter-dimensional periscopes. Mirtha watched as Bobbie-Sue touched the bark of the Tree. Oh, how delicious it would be if she could taste the saltiness of those fingers. Mirtha had not tasted anything since her imprisonment. On the Outside, however, there would be no such thing as hunger, thirst, want or need. Simply *being* would be fulfilling enough.

"I must find a way to escape this god-forsaken Prison!" she clenched her fist. "Can this girl be the key to unlocking the cellar door of physical existence?" She scratched the back of her head with a blackened fingernail until she grew tired. She would ponder the question further after getting some rest.

She hobbled over to the granite slab that was her bed, pulled the sapphider silk blankets over her shoulders and before she knew it, was asleep.

Bobbie-Sue awoke at exactly 6:16 AM. Wow, she thought, I hardly ever get up this early. She sprang out of bed, got dressed and bounded down the stairs to the kitchen where her mother was packing her lunch.

"Morning," said Ms. Viola, "my goodness, you're up early."

"Yeah," Bobbie-Sue reached over her mother's shoulder and grabbed the Cocoa Pebbles from the cabinet, "'tis quite unusual for me to be up this early,"

"And so chipper too," her mother chuckled, "keep this up and you'll get a lot done in life."

Bobbie-Sue procured a bowl, spoon, and milk. The brown crunchlets crackled as she poured the milk. "I have a world history test today," she said while chewing. "It's about Rome during the time of Jesus," she swallowed her cereal. "Don't you think it's weird for a public school to be teaching about Jesus?" She took a napkin and wiped her chin.

"Well," said her mother, "there is a difference between the historical Jesus of Nazareth and the Jesus worshipped by the Christians. One camp takes a factual approach while the other is dependent on faith."

Bobbie-Sue smiled, "You always have a way of saying things that make sense."

"Why thank you," Ms. Viola bowed, "I take much pride in my ability to distill and simplify abstract concepts."

Distill sounded like 'dill,' triggering a flashback. Bobbie-

Sue hated pickles and anything with dill in it. Her grandfather had been proud of his pickle recipe and had at least a
hundred jars stashed in his garage. He tried to get Bobbie-
Sue and her parents to taste his pickles at every opportunity,
but would always be politely refused.

One day, her father and grandfather had gone searching
the woods for old jars buried in the swampy soil. They never
came back. At around six in the evening, Ms. Viola went
looking for them only to find they had been crushed by a
fallen tree.

Years after the tragedy, Bobbie-Sue would strive to overcome her fear of the forest by venturing a bit further in each
day. By the time she was thirteen, she had nearly eliminated
her phobia. Dill still made her sick though. Her mother's
homophonic allusion to it seemed to portend something, but
Bobbie-Sue didn't know what. Perhaps the tree she had
discovered the other day could cleanse her of this bad
energy.

"There's an hour before the bus gets here," Bobbie-Sue
stood and pushed in her chair, "is it okay if I go visit my
lucky tree out in the woods?"

Her mother stared at her blankly for a moment, "I
guess," she said, "If it helps you ace your test, go for it. Just
be careful, and make sure you start heading back ten
minutes before the bus gets here."

"Don't worry, mom" Bobbie-Sue giggled, "I'll be right on
time." She slid open the back porch door and jogged off
toward the woods.

The tree looked the same as it did the day before. Bobbie-
Sue ran her fingers over the carvings. She wondered if it was
some sort of sacred tree, like the ones Buddhist monks medi-
tated under. What was on the back of it? She went around to
the side she had not yet examined.

There were characters on the back as well, including a triangular depression that stood out from the rest. She inserted her finger into the triangle. As soon as she did, she felt as if she'd gotten a static shock, but it was much more painful than any electrically charged piece of laundry. It wasn't so much physical pain as it was a jolt of emotional anguish. Over the next few minutes, she began to feel it work its way to the core of her being. She felt dirty and sick, like she had just drank a jar of pickle juice mixed with urine. She wanted to cry, to punch herself in the face, to cut herself. She felt loathing. Hatred.

"What is wrong with me?" She clutched her head. "What just happened? Am I imagining this?" She felt woozy. The world, to her, was now crawling with worms and beetles. The edges of reality were curling like an ancient manuscript on fire.

"I'll be okay," she was shivering even though it was early September. "Maybe I'm just getting my period." It was around that time anyhow. And fall was fast approaching. Perhaps it was early-onset seasonal affective disorder. "If I can make it through the day," she whispered, "I'll be a stronger person for it." She shuffled out of the forest and through the gate. The bushes that once grew green and healthy along the bottom of the fence were now black and sticky, leaves engorged with colonies of white lice.

Seven hours earlier, while Bobbie-Sue was still asleep, Mirtha came up with a plan. She now knew why Bobbie-Sue seemed so different from other beings of her dimension. The girl had strong intuition; her subconscious was linked to higher planes, such as the one Mirtha had originally come from. If she were to focus her awareness on Bobbie-Sue as she was touching the Conduit Tree, Mirtha could transmigrate into her body through the Mirrow. Then Mirtha would kill Bobbie-Sue and hitch a ride to the Outside on her soul; a free ride to Pleroma.

According to the Mirrow, Bobbie-Sue would visit the Conduit Tree before getting on the bus for school, the perfect opportunity to enter her body.

Even after Bobbie-Sue had boarded the school bus, she still felt sick. Was it her imagination, or had someone or something icky grabbed a hold of and begun to molest a spiritual/emotional fiber at the deepest level of her psyche?

The whole bus ride was an agony of defeatist thoughts bouncing off the trees rolling by. Whenever the bus stopped, her stomach lurched. Whenever a new group of kids got on, the taunting echoes of their voices crashed into the walls of her skull like wrecking balls.

What's going on in my mind?

She massaged her temples with the pads of her fingers. It's like a migraine, but it also feels like I'm going insane. It's like my dad cursing at me, beating me ... even though he never did that. Someone ... anyone ... help me!

She struggled to keep the pungent, vitriolic thoughts frothing inside her head from spilling out, praying that her body language wouldn't give away her distress.

Teddy, a flannel shirt wearing eighth grader poked his head out from the seat in front of Bobbie-Sue.

"You're making noises like a dying rat," said Teddy.

"Are you okay?"

"Yes-yes-yes!" Bobbie-Sue flapped her hand dismissively as the witch smashed her joyful memories with a sledgehammer.

"I'm fine, don't worry about me."

"O-kay ... "

Teddy retreated to his seat and popped in his ear buds.

The inside of Bobbie-Sue's mind was warm and inviting, filled with teddy bears and anime characters and ideas for drawings she could scrawl on her friend Jessie Cline's notebook while the teacher wasn't looking.

"It's a shame to have to destroy all of this," said Mirtha, "but in this case, the ends certainly justify the means. I mean, won't we both be a lot better off as part of the Outside rather than rotting away in our respective Labyrinths?" She called into existence an array of weapons with which she'd bludgeon, rend, and gut Bobbie-Sue's spirit. She'd break its teeth, bash its head into the corner of a table, cut its eyes out, and torture it until her body could no longer hold onto it. She lifted a chainsaw from the armory, revved it and began to shred everything in sight; the walls, the plush furniture, the stuffed animals, the bedspread, the pillows, all the comforting features of Bobbie-Sue's mind that made it a nice place to be. Mirtha did not stop until the room was a blizzard of animal stuffing and feathers.

All throughout the school day, Bobbie-Sue was racked with excruciating physical and emotional pain. She'd had migraines before and knew that her mother's side of the family was predisposed to them, but this time, the pain had reached an unprecedented level of agony. It was as if a troop of monkeys were tearing at the flesh of her scalp, grinding, clawing, and pounding at her skull with blunt tools, making their way to the meaty flesh of her motor cortex, hacking it up and gorging on it. It hurt to exist. Her German teacher had the face of a deer tick. Bobbie-Sue's stomach had become a lamprey mouth.

She was able to procure a pass to the nurse's office, but she had to get out of the room quick because every one of her classmates' heads were twisting off and clouds of bees were swarming from their neck holes. Bees, she remembered, flew as fast as humans ran. She could barely shuffle two feet without feeling like the floor was going to become liquid.

The hallways wriggled as she staggered to the nurse's office.

The letters on the office door burned her face.

Sitting on a cot, she dry heaved seventeen times into a sanitary bag. The nurse called her mother who picked her up in her gray minivan and brought her home.

Mirtha pumped twenty magazines of steel-jacketed AK -47 rounds into every cherished photograph and childhood memory in Bobbie-Sue's mind. She carved up her self-esteem nodule with a hacksaw and torched the pieces with a flamethrower.

At home, Bobbie-Sue, wrapped in blankets with a damp cloth on her forehead, moaned and writhed under the excruciating pain she felt in every part of her body. Her mother took her temperature, and after reading 108 on the thermometer, noticed the blood oozing from her daughter's tear ducts and called 911.

Not even Bobbie-Sue's fantasies involving boys she liked were safe from Mirtha's hedge clippers and sledgehammers. She tackled the gel-haired boys to the ground, snipped off their peckers and smashed their scrotums. Bobbie-Sue's inner-observer clasped her hands to her mouth. When would it stop? As a means of self-defense, her mind labeled Mirtha's psychological assault as a viral infection, but all the antibodies on the planet wouldn't have been enough to neutralize this particular pathogen.

On the way to the hospital, a paramedic named Stacy conversed with Bobbie-Sue.

"You're doing fine, sweetie, we're almost there."

"The-the ... " Bobbie-Sue coughed.

"What is it?" Stacy placed a hand on Bobbie-Sue's shoulder. "Talk to me, tell me what's wrong."

"The Labyrinth ..." Bobbie-Sue muttered, "I gotta ... escape ... the Labyrinth!"

"What's the labyrinth hun?" She had to suppress a giggle. "Is that a game?"

"N-no ... " Bobbie-Sue's voice had become uncharacteristically gravelly and phlegmatic. "The Labyrinth is one h-half of re ... al ... ity." She coughed, spotting her chest with bloody sputum. Her head rolled to the side. Her eyes whitened.

Even after running every test in the book, the doctors could not determine what was wrong with her. She was unresponsive, and her pulse and blood pressure were lethally high. All they could do was pack her in ice, pump her full of anti-hypertension drugs, and hope that she would make it through the night. Her mother stood by her side the whole time.

An emergency assembly was called at the school to inform the students of Bobbie-Sue's condition. The bleachers buzzed with theories. One of them was meningitis, but that was shot down in favor of beaver fever. Bobbie-Sue hung out in the woods all the time. Maybe she drank water from the wrong stream. One boy laughed at the idea, but was quickly shushed by the others. Bobbie-Sue might have been a loner, but her awkward grace at volleyball had charmed even Betsy Charles, the ringleader of the popular girls. Coach Johnson had asked Bobbie-Sue to join the volleyball team, but his invitations fell on deaf ears. Bobbie-Sue's gaze would often be fixed on something far beyond the gym ceiling. Was she communicating with her home planet? Was she daydreaming about pinball machine universes inside giant space jellyfish? Nobody knew for sure. Bobbie-Sue would always remain an enigma.

Mrs. Trotski was in the middle of explaining the situation when she got the call from Ms. Viola saying that Bobbie-Sue had passed away in the hospital.

The Principal and administrators decided to send the kids home early that day without breaking the news. They would mail letters to the parents over the weekend regarding Bobbie-Sue's fate. The parents, they figured, should be the ones to tell them. There would be an official announcement on Monday.

$$\Omega \Omega \Omega$$

The world beyond death was black and empty.

But the pain was gone!

A Presence made itself known in the blackness. It moved its fingers and wiggled its toes.

It was aware.

It felt the urge to open its eyes.

As the curtains of its eyes lifted, the first thing to enter was a beam of light reflecting off something gold and shiny. It put its hands up to its eyes and rubbed them. When it was able to focus, it saw that it was a person and that it was female. It also had a name.

"Bobbie-Sue," it said aloud. "Bobbie-Sue. Bobbie-Sue. I ... am ... Bobbie. I ... am ... Sue. I am Bobbie-Sue ... and I am alive?"

She patted herself all over and pinched the skin of her left arm. "I'm not dead," she whispered, "am I?"

All around her was black except for the floor which was made of a membranous white material. It reminded her of the puffy clouds in Super Mario Bros. 3, except that none of them were smiling. Towering above her was a golden archway adorned with turquoise jewels.

"What is this?" her heart leapt. "Where am I?" She stood for a minute and thought. "Wait a minute," she gasped. "Could it be? Am I ... am I in Heaven?" At first, she was overcome with joy. She stood silent for a few more minutes and marveled at the spectacle of the magnificent archway above her.

Then she became aware of a nagging pain in her left leg. She took a deep breath, craned her neck slowly to the left and downward. Dangling just above her ankle was a black, bulbous tumor sporting several eyeballs, hair, and claws.

She shrieked and thrashed her leg. The feeling of the eyeballs bumping against her shin immediately caused her to stop. She realized the thing was attached to her, and felt queasy. Before she could turn to hurl, the thing spoke.

"Bobbie-Sue!" its voice rumbled like dried nicotine mustard being squeezed out of a whoopee cushion.

Bobbie-Sue dismissed the voice as a cruel trick of her imagination. She began to hobble toward the arch, making the utmost effort to ignore the growth on her leg that had definitely not just spoken to her.

"Bobbie-Sue! Listen to me. I thought I was doing you a favor."

She continued to ignore the misfirings of her decayed synapses and trudged ever closer to the arch.

"I was trying to liberate us from the confines of flesh. I wanted to deliver us both into a world where we could find peace and harmony and fullness. But apparently this isn't it. It seems like this is just some stereotypical storybook depiction of Christian Heaven."

"Please shut up ... please shut up ... please shut up ..." Bobbie-Sue wanted to curl up and die again.

"I'm sorry, okay? Look, let me start by introducing

myself. I'm Mirtha. I was born in a higher dimension than your own. I was cast out of my home and trapped in a glass sunflower. I escaped by binding my spirit to yours through the Conduit Tree, you know, the one in your backyard. That thing is like a connection point between dimensions. The boundaries between them get kind of blurred at places like that, so ..."

"Will you just shut the fuck up?!" Bobbie-Sue ejected with a force she never thought herself capable of. "Please let God be on the other side of that arch," she whimpered. "Maybe He can help me get rid of this growth on my leg that won't stop talking to me."

"Listen," Mirtha snapped. "God isn't here. This is not the Divine Realm. It's an imitation meant to confuse post-mortal entities and dissuade them from searching for the next highest level. I know this because if we were really Outside of the Labyrinth, there would be no more pain, no more ugliness and no reason to quarrel. On the Outside, everyone and everything simply *is* in a state of eternal placidity without need or want of anything."

"I thought I told you to shut up!" her voice cracked as if she were about to cry.

"Fine, fine," Mirtha grumbled. "But since we're stuck together, shouldn't we at least call a truce and try to cooperate. We both want the same thing, right?"

"How could we want the same thing?" Salty tears stung Bobbie-Sue's eyes. "You're just a part of whatever disease killed me. You're an infection that can talk. Why should I believe anything you say? As soon as I see God, I'm gonna have him freeze you off like a wart. That's all you are: a wart, a pimple that needs to be popped!"

"But ..." Mirtha, for perhaps the first time in her life, felt ready to cry. What is this feeling? She wondered. Since when do I have feelings? I must have feelings now. Otherwise, how could my feelings be hurt? She became silent and remained that way as Bobbie-Sue trudged across the threshold of the golden archway and into whatever type of false splendor awaited her on the other side.

"What the ...?" Neither Bobbie-Sue nor Mirtha were prepared for what awaited them beyond the arch. Floating in a gulf of blackness were four gigantic human heads orbiting a colossal squid watering a tomato garden. The squid wore a crown of centipedes and millipedes inter-twined in a double helix formation. Sitting atop the Squid's head was a red-haired boy scribbling in a notebook.

I see, Mirtha thought. This must be the realm of the Demiurge, the false god who created Bobbie-Sue's universe. He's probably responsible for the creation of a whole bunch of universes. Even so, the one we're in now is just one of a trillion within the molecular structure of a goat's penis or something. The Labyrinth doesn't end, but escape *is* possi-ble. Don't ask me how I know. Maybe it's a matter of persis-tence. Or luck. Or the realization that causality is dependent on luck. It's a roll of the cosmic dice whether we exist or not at any given time. Makes it seem kind of wonderful to be alive if you look at it that way. Here, in this moment, we have a breathtaking view of a cosmos in action. Someone inside one of those tomatoes probably thinks that squid over there is God.

The squid wrapped a tentacle around a tomato, plucked it from the vine, stuffed it in its beak, chewed and swallowed.

I wonder why the squid chose to plant the garden in the first place, Mirtha continued to ponder. Perhaps it was for the same reason I pilfered the Mirrow from the glassanthill or why Bobbie-Sue would choose to go to college: self-suste-nance, the drive to better the quality of one's life.

Out of the darkness, a sperm whale emerged. The squid

inserted a tentacle into the bottoms of each of the four floating heads. Their faces grimaced and the centipede/millipede crown began to revolve. The squid flared the rest of its tentacles, revealing its beak. Inside the beak, a ball of light grew larger and brighter. The sperm whale dove toward the squid, and the squid launched the ball of light at the whale. The ball singed the whale's face. The whale recoiled, but quickly regained its bearings and prepared for a second attack.

As the whale approached, the mouths of the floating heads opened and spewed clouds of greenish-yellow gas. The gas made its way into the whale's blowhole. The whale scrunched its face, did a one-eighty and swam off at full speed.

Bobbie-Sue felt as though several pieces were missing from the puzzle her mind needed to reconstruct in order to understand what had just happened.

"What did I just see?" She put her hand to her head and sat down cross-legged on the puffy, cloud-like terrain. "Where are we? How did we end up here? Is that what God looks like? A squid? You've got to be kidding me." She slapped her forehead with her open palm.

"That's not God," said Mirtha. "It's just a universe-creator. Many such beings exist on various planes of the Labyrinth. Humans may be one of them. The God behind *everything*, the God of the Outside is incomprehensible from this vantage point. He cannot be directly observed by mortal or post-mortal beings. To even name Him doesn't do Him justice. He's a pluralized existence that has always been and will continue to be. In His realm, there is no time, no cause and effect, no end, and no beginning. He just *Is*. Those who reach His level become part of a boundless existence that *Is* and is *Good*. That's all we can really say about Him."

Bobbie-Sue had tuned out midway through Mirtha's diatribe. It was clear that the squid, the floating heads, and the centipedes were not Gods. But how would she, with this sentient tumor attached to her ankle, be able to find a path to the realm of the so-called 'real God?'

"I know what you're thinking," said Mirtha. "I'm a part of your soul after all. We both have the same goal in mind. So whaddya say? You wanna let bygones be bygones and search for the realm of God together?"

Bobbie-Sue rolled her eyes and reluctantly glanced at the thing riding her ankle. Its eyes glistened with a sort of humility she would have never expected to find in such a nightmarish creature.

"Alright," she finally said. "Since we're stuck together and we both have the same destination, we might as well cooperate."

The abomination seemed to smile. "Okay," she chirped, "then let's be off."

Bobbie-Sue rose to her feet.

"Let's try going inside one of those heads," said Mirtha, "the one with the dumb expression should be a good place to start."

ΩΩΩ

Fiiiiiiinkleeeeeeer! The dopey-looking head whispered, sending a gust of putrid breath crashing into Bobbie-Sue's nostrils as she mounted the summit of its lower lip. She and Mirtha learned quickly that the world within was called the Finkler Dimension. The Finklerians were nude, hairless ape-like beings with ambiguous genitalia who were more than eager to assist traveling strangers. All they wanted in return was for Bobbie-Sue and Mirtha to become their buddies. The only problem was that the Finklerians were predisposed to not accepting responsibility for their misdeeds. If a Finklerian was accused of doing something inappropriate, they would dodge the blame by making an evasive statement like 'where's the proof?' or 'but it's not fair!'

The oniony stench that hung everywhere suggested that Finklerians had no concept of personal hygiene. In fact, they needed daily reminders to bathe themselves. Instructions on how to properly wet, wash, and rinse their bodies were tacked to the walls of their dwellings by the Staff, a minority race whose intelligence far surpassed that of the child-like Finklerians.

Bobbie-Sue and Mirtha searched high and low for a path to God, but all they could find were rows upon rows of televisions showing the same episode of what the Finklerians called 'Sim-sims.' Sim-sims was essentially a dumbed-down, distorted version of The Simpsons. As they passed ten or twenty of rows of TVs, they noticed that the Finklerians would watch the same episode over and over and laugh at the same jokes every time, despite having heard them thousands, perhaps millions of times. The only one not laughing was a red-haired boy sitting next to a particularly chubby Finklerian, sketching something on Bristol board.

"Okay," Mirtha said to Bobbie-Sue after they reached the fifty-seventh row of Finklerian TV watchers, "I think I've had enough of this dimension, how about you?"

"Same." Bobbie-Sue didn't really give a shit either way.

They exited via Finkler's left ear and made their way across the stretch of ribbon that connected the heads to one another.

The adjacent head was even more bald and childlike than Finkler had been. This head had buck teeth and black marble eyes magnified by lenses thick enough to be part of a cutting-edge space telescope.

As soon as they passed the threshold of its ear canal, it became clear to Bobbie-Sue that this world was familiar. It wasn't as if she'd been there before, but she swore she had read about it or heard it described through the pop-culture grapevine.

They had entered a smoldering volcano. A stocky man with forests of curly hair covering his head and feet stood on a ledge overlooking a lava pit. A decrepit weasel of a man was crawling over a heap of rocks behind the hairy one, probably attempting to sneak up behind him and catch him off guard.

"Give me back my precious!" the scrawny man snarled as he leapt onto the hairy man's back and tried to pry a golden ring from his finger. The two wrestled and traded blows. After both had sustained many cuts and bruises, the wretched man bit off the hairy man's finger and fell with it and the ring into the lava pit.

Then the world switched channels as if the whole thing had been just a giant TV show. Now it showed a face, the face of the Dimension itself tossing its head back and laughing as if it was some sort of white, chubby, child version of Ray Charles.

"This is just weird," Bobbie-Sue shuddered.

"We should get out of here soon," Mirtha jiggled one of her eyestalks. "But where is the exit? I don't see any way out. It feels like we're stuck in inside a TV."

"Maybe we can change the channel," Bobbie-Sue said, half sardonically.

"Doubtful," said Mirtha. "I feel like this is one of those Lotus-Eater machines ... meaning we're really not here. Our minds are just being fed information telling us that we're here. I don't know if we'll ever be able return to the outside world again."

"You know what?" Bobbie-Sue's tone had sharpened to a fine point. "I think you're full of shit with your talk about a realm of pure goodness outside of this one. I think this is actually Hell and that you being attached to my leg and leading me on this wild goose chase is my eternal punishment. I should've known I wouldn't be going to Heaven. I don't know what I did to deserve this. Maybe it's because I never 'accepted Jesus' when my bible thumper friends tried to convert me. Maybe they were right. I should have accepted Jesus. I should have listened to them."

Mirtha thought for a moment. "They meant well," she said finally, "but they never truly understood what they were talking about. Salvation has nothing to do with what you do or don't do in the physical world. Upon death, everyone is saved. I just don't understand why we ended up here instead of there."

"Maybe the weight of two souls is too much to allow either of them to enter the real Heaven if there is one," Bobbie-Sue spat. "Maybe your little plan to stow away aboard my soul blew up in your face. And you didn't see it coming even though you're supposedly from some 'higher dimension.' Face it, you messed up big time ... and you dragged *me* into it. You're despicable."

Mirtha said nothing. She knew, with absolute certainty that Bobbie-Sue was right. The girl had extra-sensory capabilities after all. It came down to a problem of mass. Two souls joined together were too heavy to escape the Labyrinth's gravity. That explained why God had intended each individual body to contain only one soul.

The channels began to cycle rapidly. There was a scene featuring a prepubescent boy leaning over a counter, talking to a sporty-looking young adult twirling a lanyard around his finger. He addressed the boy as 'Yasher.'

"Yasher." Mirtha recognized the boy's face. It was the same as that of the floating head.

The channel flipped to a scene featuring two middle aged women on a school bus. They were baby-talking to a deformed boy in a wheelchair. His head moved around at random and his mouth opened and closed, revealing rows of jagged, white teeth.

"Ricky-Ricky Rollins!" One of the bus ladies cooed.

Ricky's jaws clamped down on the fleshy part of her hand.

"Uh-uh ..." said the one whose hand wasn't currently being chewed, "no biteys, Ricky, no biteys."

Bobbie-Sue and Mirtha noticed a teenage boy sitting two seats away with his head against the window. The gray of his headphones contrasted sharply with his poofy red hair. He was staring at a group of birds perched on the boughs of a barren tree.

"Who is that?" Bobbie-Sue squinted to get a better look "I feel like I've seen him before."

"I dunno," said Mirtha, "He could be a phantom of someone Yasher once knew. Or maybe he's a wandering thought-presence that appears in all of them."

"What makes you say that?" Bobbie-Sue no longer had enough energy to be angry. Her emotional pendulum had settled on complacency.

"I'm pretty sure I saw him watching TV with the Finkle-rians. And wasn't that him riding atop that orange squid's head? He's been in every place we've visited. I'm surprised you didn't notice him sooner."

Bobbie-Sue thought about it for a moment. "Now that you mention it, I do remember seeing him, or at least his hair. It was kind of comforting, like his presence was protecting me while we traveled across the ribbon."

"Perhaps we both knew him during some other lifetime," said Mirtha, "but our memories of him keep getting erased by God so that we don't have to continually bear the burden of searching for him with each life we live."

"Anyway," Bobbie-Sue shuddered, "I just hope we can get out of here soon."

As if on cue, the scene shifted again. This time, they

were in some sort of basement lounge. Teenagers were playing video games, ping-pong and doing yoga. Sitting at the far edge of the ping pong table was the red-headed boy. He was drawing something on a piece of computer paper.

Bobbie-Sue leaned over his shoulder to get a glimpse of what he was drawing. It was a smiley face with rows of teeth that resembled those of the wheelchair boy from the previous scene. Its eyebrows were upturned, giving it a sort of guilty expression. Coming from its mouth was a speech bubble that said; 'HEEY!' Beneath the face, was the statement; 'I AM DICK!'

"I am Dick?" Bobbie-Sue clasped her chin between her thumb and forefinger. "That's sort of like 'Ricky,' the kid in the wheelchair."

"Yes," said Mirtha, "and Yasher's first name is also Richard. I read it on a piece of paper that man twirling his keys was holding."

"But what does it all mean?" Bobbie-Sue rubbed her forehead, "these dimensions are full of so many weird signs and symbols. I just can't wrap my head around it."

"To be honest, neither can I," said Mirtha. "This is the first time in all my life I can say I'm stumped. If I had the Mirrow with me, I could tell you the answer right away but alas—"

"You got greedy and screwed us both."

"That was—" Mirtha felt flustered, "I'm sure we'll find the answers as soon as we solve the puzzle of the spatial loop we've got ourselves stuck in. Let's just allow it to play out and see where it takes us. Maybe things will sort themselves out on their ..."

The world took Bobbie-Sue and Mirtha through the smiley face's mouth. Everything went black for a few minutes, and then another scene came into focus. The red-haired boy was seated cross-legged in the atrium of a different building, apparently a school. He wore an army surplus jacket and was drawing comic strips in a blank book bound with gator skin. When his pencil got dull, he sharpened it and brushed the shavings onto the floor.

Bobbie-Sue and Mirtha crouched behind him to catch a glimpse of his work. He was drawing the same smiley face, but from a side-view angle. A starship was flying into its mouth dodging wavy lines labeled 'stinky,' with an arrow.

Bobbie-Sue giggled. This was the first time she had felt amusement since entering this post-mortem world of strangeness. Mirtha was laughing too, even though she had no mouthparts.

A yellow short bus pulled up to the atrium and the door opened. A young-ish driver beckoned the boy to come aboard. The boy packed up his drawing supplies, flew out the door and bounded up the steps of the bus. Bobbie-Sue and Mirtha followed him.

As the bus passed a Burger King, a Sunoco and other staples of suburbia, the boy and the driver conversed about religion.

"So," said the bus driver, "have you decided whether or not you're going to accept Jesus Christ as your Lord and savior?"

"Uh ..." the boy was clearly not interested in blindly accepting Jesus, but decided to play along just to humor the driver. "Yeah," said the boy, "I definitely believe Jesus was a great man and had a lot of great things to say."

"But, do you accept him as your Lord and savior though?" the driver asked.

"Well," the boy curled a lock of hair around his finger, "I think Jesus already knows that I try to do good for humanity. Like how I hold the door open for people and go out of my way to stand up for those low-functioning kids that Billy usually targets."

"But good works are not enough to save you from Hell,"

the bus driver pressed, "only Jesus can save you from the Lake of Fire, and I won't let you burn, Brian. I am here to tell you about the good news of His teachings and that only through Him can you be saved."

"But what if I don't believe in Hell?" Brian watched a squirrel dart behind a tree. "Will I still go there if I don't believe?"

"Oh, absolutely yes," the driver cut a hard left, "your disbelief in Hell is Satan trying to trick you. He's trying to steer you away from the light of God. Don't listen to him Brian, trust me. Or, more importantly, put all of your trust in Jesus Christ."

After several minutes of tense silence, Brian finally said "I'll think about it, but for right now, I'm gonna listen to my music."

"Okay," said the driver, "there's no hurry. Jesus can wait for as long as you live. Even if you declare you undying trust in Him on your deathbed, you can still be saved."

But Brian had completely tuned out. "Fuck Christ" by the Satanists blared from his headphones.

All the while, Bobbie-Sue and Mirtha watched and listened. With each passing moment, they became more and more acquainted with Brian's character, thought processes, and defining traits.

The bus pulled into the parking lot of a much larger building; another high school. The driver opened the door and of course, before Brian exited, went on his whole spiel about Jesus and salvation. As soon as Brian stepped off the bus and took in the scenery, the open doors of the school building, the kids wearing backpacks going to and fro, the fresh air, the freedom, the *true* salvation, his pupils dilated with joy and he felt as though he had ascended to *his* version of Heaven.

These were Brian's memories, but Bobbie-Sue and

Mirtha were experiencing them as if they were their own. They grasped intuitively that Brian had already been through Hell. The four floating heads were demonic presences from his past that still lingered his mind. He drew those demons, like Richard Yasher/Dick/Ricky Rollins in order to make light of them, to soothe the wounds they had inflicted upon his soul. But here, at this ordinary-looking high school, he felt he was in Heaven. He would get to be amongst kids as bright and intelligent as he was; free from the torment of macho street thugs and bullies who had nothing better to do than pick on innocent girls with schizophrenia and nerdy aspies like him.

This high school was the Divine Light at the end of Hell's Tunnel through which he had crawled on his belly, collecting stretch marks and fat from medications that stimulated his appetite centers and made him hungry twenty-four hours a day. His brain had been lasered by the surveillance systems of the all-seeing Eyeball, diced by the surgical tools of the Cultural Normalization Facility hidden beneath the hills of Eastern Pennsylvania. He had been psychologically conditioned to ask permission from authority figures to move from one room to another. To him, being allowed to attend a public high school, which might have seemed mundane or even dreadful to the average kid, was like ascending to the highest circle of God's Kingdom.

Bobbie-Sue and Mirtha felt warm waves of bliss emanating from his heart. His soul, at that moment was not a twisted blob of skin, but a baby wrapped in his favorite blanket, 'born again' so to speak. Bobbie-Sue felt the mass of cancerous flesh that was Mirtha, slide off of her ankle. The mass sizzled on the concrete, steamed and became dry. A crack appeared in one of the malignant lumps. Out of the crack, a butterfly emerged with wings that seemed to connect with the rays of the sun. The sunlight, Mirtha's wings, and the light from Brian's heart joined and formed a triangular sail. This sail would carry them all the way to the Outside.

"Grab on to me," the Mirtha butterfly said to Bobbie-Sue, "let us exit this place together,"

"Right." Bobbie-Sue wrapped her fingers around Mirtha's leg.

A wind began to blow from beneath them and they were carried up into the sky towards the sun. They became one with the rays of the sun; transformed into pure light. The mass of light retreated into the sun.

As soon as the light vanished, a magnolia petal fell from the sky and landed near Brian's feet. He took the petal and stuck it between the pages of a book he had with him.

The book was a collection of poetry, drama, and prose by William Butler Yeats. On the page marked by the petal were these words:

I think all happiness depends on having the energy to assume the mask of some other self, that all joyous or creative life is a rebirth as something not oneself, something created in a moment and perpetually renewed in playing a game like that of a child where one loses the infinite pain of self-realization, a grotesque or solemn painted face put on that one may hide from the terrors of judgment, an imaginative Saturnalia that makes one forget reality. Perhaps all the sins and energies of the world are but the world's flight from an infinite blinding beam (253-254).

FROGBABY

I was born without a brain or spine, yet I control the cosmos. I make the sun rise and set. I cause the moon to wax and wane. I set the planets in their orbits. I invented gravity and all the laws of physics. Yet, I know nothing. I feel neither pain nor joy. I am not alive in the traditional sense, but I am better at living than you. In order to be like me, you'd have to stick your neck under a guillotine or blow your head off with a shotgun. I don't advise taking either of these actions. A mind is a terrible thing to waste, that is, unless you never had one to begin with. Good times create vacuums as they pass by. One could say to have experienced anything at all is life's greatest tragedy. Time is responsible for the existence of beginnings and endings. To be born dead is to never know misery. The only reason people fear death is because they've been given a taste of life. Upon death, all reverts to the simplicity of unconsciousness. I was granted this privilege right from the start. I'll be waiting **here** *at no place in particular for you to join me.*

The doctors said it was anencephaly, a rare condition where

the brain and spinal cord never developed. Sheila's baby came out looking like a frog: two protruding eyes encased in pockets of pink flesh, a nose and a mouth, but no cranium. They warned her that the baby's appearance might be disturbing, but she maintained that she wanted to see him before they carted him off to be incinerated. They dumped the frogbaby into her arms without so much as a piece of linen to cover him. She rocked him and sang a lullaby her mother had written to the tune of an old blues song. 'I just can't keep from cryin' sometimes.,' the song went. Her tears splashed onto his healthy-looking cheeks making it seem like his frog-eyes where shedding tears of their own. She and her husband Dan named him Ryan. For lack of a better reason, they picked the name because it rhymed with 'cryin'.'

Not even two minutes later, an army of nurses appeared and said it was time to say goodbye. They literally had to pry Ryan from Sheila's arms. She howled and buried her face in Dan's nylon jacket as they dropped the beautiful boy in a box and sealed the lid.

Was God preoccupied with other things? Dan stroked Sheila's stringy hair. *Does He realize how much pain we're in right now?*

As an amateur theologian, Dan had concluded early on that God, like the human race, was imperfect. This ran totally counter to Biblical tradition, but it made so much sense to Dan. Astrophysicists affirmed that the universe had to have been uneven at the moment of the Big Bang for matter to coagulate into planets, stars, and galaxies. From a mystical standpoint, this irregularity was not accidental: God had made things this way on purpose. Without evil, intelligent beings wouldn't be able to appreciate goodness. The interplay of positive and negative stimuli on the human psyche over time is what generated reality and allowed for free will. But as Dan watched his son's body being wheeled off for cremation, he began to lament the idea of the universe being imperfect for the sake of sentient creatures knowing joy.

Is this really necessary? He swallowed what felt like a walnut lodged in his throat. *Is this a game to you, sitting up there on your golden throne, spinning a roulette wheel to see whose turn it is to be sacrificed for the greater good? I guess my son's number just happened to come up, huh? What does one little brat matter? He won't miss taking his first breath, feeling his mother's embrace or wrapping his tiny hand around his old man's finger. Infants can't retain memories, so it's all good, right?*

I don't mean to be a sore loser. Everyone has to lose sometime. But why not kill me instead? Have some street thug gun me down or let a truck squash me like a pancake. Why my son? He didn't have enough time to say his first word let alone win the Nobel Prize or commit mass genocide. I've done plenty of dumb things in my forty-six years. Taking me out of the picture would rid the world of a hell of a lot of stupidity. But I guess that's not how it works. Maybe it is all a lottery set in motion at the beginning of time. But what do I know? My perceptual organs probably can't begin to comprehend the reasons why. At this point, I feel like I'm the one without a brain or spinal cord.

Dan sighed and squeezed Sheila as tight as he could.

The silence was broken by the *clock, clock* of business shoes on the linoleum floor. A doctor approached the huddled couple and informed them of some papers they needed to sign. Dan held Sheila close as the three of them shuffled off to some other part of the labyrinthine hospital complex to do paperwork.

We are the ones who are One and All. We exist behind empty mirrors. We pour the tea for two as well as three. When four comes around, we hide. Why? Because we're scared of differ-

entiation. We are only content when things stay the same. Change frightens us more than anything. Change is the nature of the place where the Outsiders live: the Ones who are ones unto themselves, not all, but Many ... fragmented ... alone ... resigned to playing chess by themselves, stacking decks of cards and cheating at solitaire ... They are the ones you've got to watch out for. They will steal the sunlight from your day. Beware the parasites of crudest excrement. They will leech everything you have built. They will devour your sympathy and thrive on your guilt ...

Three weeks later, Sheila returned to her job as a substitute teacher's aide and Dan went back to writing. Weary of theology, he decided to switch gears and publish young adult fiction. Through these books, he hoped to introduce surrealism and the avant-garde to audiences between the ages of twelve and eighteen. For the past few weeks, he had been working on a book called *Lily and Abe Visit Mazgua City*: a story of two frogs who venture far beyond the boundaries of their pond and end up in the capital city of planet Mazgua. The following is an excerpt from the book:

Lily and Abe stood among the crowd in the city center weeping for a wounded pterodactyl. Lily offered the avian dinosaur an apple from her lunch bag, but it refused. Instead, it beseeched the frogs to fulfill its final wish: unlock the vault hidden in the laboratory beneath the abandoned city library. There, they would find the pterodactyl's unhatched eggs. Upon hatching, the babies would avenge their mother's death by flying up to the Castle on the Hill and slaying the Owl who observes the actions and thoughts of everyone in the city.

"Not to worry, Madame Pterodactyl. Ace Detectives

Abe and Lily are on the case!" Abe saluted.

"That's *Lily and Abe, Private Amphibians*, and don't you forget it!" Lily kicked Abe with her hind leg.

"Ouch!" Abe's tongue jolted out of his mouth involuntarily.

"Thank you so much young ones," the Pterodactyl took in a belabored breath. "I'm ... sure ... the Dino ... Gods ... will re ... ward ... you ..." It exhaled and its body slackened as if a volcano had just been removed from its chest.

"Let's go, Abel," Lily shut the Pterodactyl's eyelids and leapt into the window of a maglev bus. "We've got work to do."

"I told you not to call me that, *Lilith*." Abe followed, but almost got his foot caught in the window as it closed.

A pungent smell hit the frogs' olfactory centers as they forced open the rusted front door of the library.

"Peeyoo! What reeks in here?" Abe held his nose.

"Smells to me like dead mice or bats or something." Lily was breathing only through her mouth, which made her speech sound nasal.

"Why won't the city government do something about this?"

"The Owl *is* the city government, remember? I'm sure he had banked on everyone forgetting about this place. If his panoptic vision were to alert him of a possible intruder, he would most likely intervene personally."

"Intruders like us."

"That's why we need to find the eggs fast."

"Agreed."

While Lily searched for an entrance to the secret lab, Abe browsed the shelves for good reading material.

"Abe! Quit goofing around and help me look."

"In a minute, Lily," he picked up a dusty tome filled with blank pages. As soon as he flipped to the last page, a shadow jumped out and cast a spell which transformed him into a lobster. Lily laughed, but Abe was none too happy about it. They continued to search. Perhaps when they finally found the lab, they could procure a serum to change Abe back into a frog.

In the children's section, Lily came across a cubbyhole guarded by a black Queen chess piece. When she touched it, the world began to slow down and speed up at random intervals. Her emotions cycled like crazy:

GIGGLEHAPPYTFUNTIMES ....
hahahahahahahahahaha!!!!
Deeeppprrreeesssiiiooonnn ...
MANICSUPERSANICGINnTANIC!!!!
mel ... an ... cho ... ly ... imokayimokayimokayimokayim ...
okay? ...

Before she could get a grip on herself, a leathery mass crashed through the ceiling and squashed the Queen, missing Lily by a millimeter. It was a diplodocus. It roared at the top of its lungs. The frog and lobster covered their auditory appendages.

"Where did this thing come from?" shouted Lily.

"You want me to go and get some?" Abe couldn't hear a thing over the diplodocus' incessant roaring. "Get some of what?"

"What I said was ..."

The diplodocus' roars carried inflections of pain. It must have broken its leg in the fall.

Suddenly, the ground began to vibrate.

The diplodocus hushed up and craned its neck toward the hole it had made in the ceiling.

Lily and Abe peered through the hole with a great deal of hesitation. The situation was worse than they ever could've imagined. A flaming asteroid was hurtling toward the Earth.

"Of course," Lily's flesh was still quivering from the psychosis induced by the chess piece. "Asteroids naturally follow dinosaurs. It's the way the world works, I suppose."

The asteroid smashed into the library, bathing everything in a blaze of light and heat.

Next thing Abe and Lily knew, they were home at the pond, but something about it was different. A concrete bridge now spanned from bank to bank. A battalion of indigenous people stood on one side protesting a pink-robed wizard on the other.

"No more blood!" The Indigents hurled their spears. Nine of them missed, but the tenth's spear slid through the wizard's heart like a javelin through gelatin.

The wizard burst into flames and burned down the false scenery revealing that Lily and Abe had never left the library. There was no hole in the ceiling, no dinosaur, and no asteroid: only papers and manila folders strewn everywhere.

"Whew! It was just a mirage," Lily clasped her hands and thanked Pwap, the goddess of fortune in Frogtoadian mythology.

While Lily had been indisposed, Abe had dumped the contents of a filing cabinet onto the floor.

"Oh, good, you're awake," he clicked his mandibles. "I've found a way to access the secret laboratory. This paper here says we need to find an ivory flute hidden in a lock box somewhere in this library."

Great, Lily thought. *More locked boxes and probably*

more hallucinatory death trips. She shuddered.

It was an icy Friday evening at the beginning of February. Sheila stood by Dan's side as he read the incomplete manuscript of *Abe And Lily Visit Mazgua City* to teens with cancer at the same hospital where the couple had lost Ryan. Dan had meant to finish the book that week, but the emotional gravity well that hung above his head 24/7 had warped his sleep schedule. It tranquilized him during the day and radiated paranoia as he lay in bed. His daily meal of fast food and cheap rum and cola didn't help his condition either.

Kids from grades seven through twelve sat on the floor sharing candy hearts and giggling between fits of coughing. The air tasted like sugar and sickness. Dan might have burst into tears at any moment, but he wrestled the weakness from his eyes. He needed to maintain a sunny disposition for the sake of the kids.

"After searching the library for hours," he read, "Lily finally found the ivory flute. Turns out, a mouse had swiped it from the lock box and was carrying it around in its teeth. Lily cornered the mouse, snatched the flute and played Yankee Doodle. At the other end of the stacks, Abe reached to grab a book on frog anatomy. But before he could get his claws on it, the shelf retreated into the wall and slid sideways.

"Dag nabbit," he clacked his claws in frustration. "Just when I found something Mom wouldn't let me read. Hey, Lily!" he shouted as loud as his crustacean vocal cords would let him. "The entrance to the lab is over here!"

"Coming!"

She hopped from book pile to book pile, toppling them in the process.

The kids seemed to be enjoying the book. Their eyes were wider than any that Sheila had ever seen; except for maybe frog eyes. *What would Ryan have thought of his father's stories had he lived? Were there any instances of Frogbabies surviving birth? Even living to adulthood?* She'd never seen a full grown Frogman or woman, so she assumed it wasn't possible for them to live outside the womb.

I kept him alive though, she thought ... *at least for a little bit. While he was in my womb, he absorbed nutrients from whatever I ate and drank. He was safe, warm, and well fed despite being unconscious. Is consciousness really all that great of a thing? If you're snug, secure, and alive, why ask for anything more? I didn't choose to be born conscious. Look what this awareness has brought me: a cloud of misery that trails behind me like a fart, everywhere I go. Who's to say that consciousness is what makes human beings special? Frogbabies could probably live fulfilling lives if we could find a way of keeping them alive.*

That reminded Sheila of her colleague Mary who was out on maternity leave. Last Sheila had heard, Mary was having contractions and was due to start pushing any day.

I wonder if she's had her baby by now.

She took out her phone and logged into Facebook. She dug through her notifications, but couldn't find anything. She browsed Mary's news feed, but found no new information since her husband had posted about her going into contractions that morning.

Something glinted in her peripheral vision. She looked up and saw that one of the kids was staring at her through thick glasses. It was a boy around age thirteen. He looked like he wanted her to come over and talk to him. Her mothering instinct kicked in and she padded along the outskirts of the circle of children to where the boy was sitting. His eyes were like signed baseballs in a glass case.

"Is everything okay?" Sheila touched his shoulder with the pads of her fingers.

The boy said nothing, but held up his hands, which were cupped around something.

"What is it? Let me see," Sheila smiled.

The boy lifted his fingers a teeny bit.

Something sprang from his hands and landed on the linoleum.

A group of girls shrieked and Dan stopped reading.

"It's okay," Sheila made sure to keep a smile plastered on her face. "It's just a frog. I'll get it."

As soon as she went to scoop up the amphibian, it leapt onto the shoulder of a girl in a pink bandana. The girl flinched and the frog leapt out of the room and continued jumping until it was ten feet down the hall.

"Sorry about that, guys," Sheila's face was beginning to hurt from fake-smiling. "Keep reading, Dan, it's just this boy's pet that got loose, I'll rescue it."

Everyone laughed except for the boy, who looked like he was about to cry.

"Anyway," Dan chuckled. "The stairway leading to the lab was completely dark ..."

Sheila scanned the hallway but couldn't find the frog anywhere. She was about to give up when she saw something that made her freeze in place. Two men clad in head-to-toe protective gear were carting a metal box into an elevator marked AUTHORIZED PERSONNEL ONLY. Before the doors could shut, the frog jumped into the elevator.

A few seconds later, the doors reopened. The men had killed the frog and one of them held it by its hind leg.

"The sterility of elevator B has been compromised," the other one said into a walkie-talkie. "We're gonna need a scrub team in here before we can proceed."

"Copy that," said the voice on the other end. The men left for some other part of the building, leaving the elevator wide open.

Something stirred inside of Sheila: something that had been gnawing at her subconscious ever since Ryan's death. *There's something important down there. Wherever that elevator goes, I need to go. And that box. Something's odd about the size of that box.* She felt a gust of February wind tear at her heart even though there were no windows nearby. It blew harder and harder until it lifted her off the ground and pushed her into the elevator. *What the hell am I doing?* She mashed the 'door close' button.

Though Dan wondered what was taking Sheila so long, he continued reading to the kids:

"Lily fashioned a torch by duct taping scraps of loose-leaf paper to a meter stick and igniting them with a lighter found in the 'lost items' bin. A draft of cold air clawed at their faces as they stepped over the threshold of the hidden staircase.

"As they descended, all they could hear was the rattling of Abe's carapace, the *plink-plink* of ceiling condensation, and a barely-audible series of grunts like a demon gorging on a fresh cadaver."

Safe inside the elevator, Sheila pushed a button outlined in crimson labeled: SUB BASEMENT 2.

As the elevator plummeted, she could see her breath turning to ice. She began to shiver. *The box,* she thought, *there's something in that box I need to see.* She fingered the latch. The elevator had passed the fifth floor. She'd be at her destination soon. Who knew what awaited her at the bottom. Her heart thumped against her sternum as she undid the latch. White smoke hissed from the box as she lifted the lid.

"The room at the bottom of the stairs was so drafty, it blew out the torch," Dan read. "Lily tried blowing on it, but the flames refused to relight. She groped the wall in search of a light switch. Finding nothing, she inched forward hesitantly. Her heart was beating in her throat pouch.

"What's that sound?" said Abe scuttling along by her left foot.

"I dunno." Lily stopped and listened. "It sounds like ... breathing?"

It was faint, but the frog and lobster could tell that something large and alive was aspirating in the center of the room.

"Who's there?" Lily was too scared to be self-conscious of the tremor in her voice.

There was no response, just the same rhythmic breathing. It was as if the thing, whatever it was, was sleeping.

"Hey, I got an idea." The tone of Abe's voice suggested mischief.

Before Lily could stop him, the lobster leapt forward and pinched the flank of whatever was sleeping in the middle of the room.

The thing stirred and snorted.

Abe jumped back.

A light clicked on."

It took about five seconds for the smoke to dissipate and the contents of the box to become visible. Two marbles glinted among the smoke. Sheila jumped and her head hit the ceiling. It was a Frogbaby. Another one just like Ryan. She collapsed in a heap on the floor and began to sob.

Dan glanced up from the book to check for any sign of Sheila. Still nothing. He continued to read:

"Curled up on a throw rug was the same diplodocus Lily had hallucinated about when she touched the chess piece. It craned its neck to stare at the frog and lobster.

"You woke me up, you twits." The diplodocus' breath stank of cockroaches and mold rot.

"You don't have to call us names," Lily put her hands on her hips. "I'm sorry we woke you up, but we're here for a reason."

"And what reason is that?" The diplodocus rolled its eyes.

"We need to find a safe."

"A safe, eh?" The diplodocus chuckled. "What's in it? Anything good?"

"I don't believe that's any of your business," she said, sticking out her tongue which came within an inch of the diplodocus' nose.

"Fine, then. If you don't wanna tell me, perhaps I won't tell you *my* little secret," the diplodocus' mouth curled up into a toothless grin.

"Wait a minute," Lily waved her finger, "you know something, don't you? About the safe, I mean."

"I don't know what's in it," the diplodocus guffawed. "If you tell me what you think you might find in there, I can give you an educated guess as to where the safe *might* be. That's all."

"Don't play games with me, dinosaur," Lily sighed. "Okay, fine. We believe there's a safe in this laboratory containing the unhatched eggs of a pterodactyl we met in

Mazgua City. She was dying. She wanted us to find her babies so that they could defeat the Owl and avenge her death."

"The Owl, you say?" The diplodocus turned to face the wall. "I was hoping this day would come: when a group of youngsters fed up with the Owl's invasion of everyone's privacy would band together and put a stop to him."

When Sheila regained the courage to face the dead child in the box, she checked the tag wrapped around its foot. 'Margaret Elizabeth Thallman,' it read. Thallman was the name of Mary Richardson's husband. This was her baby.

"Mary, I'm so sorry." Sheila's hand shook uncontrollably as she reached out to touch the corpse's tiny pink foot.

"The diplodocus cleared his throat," Dan continued.

"The Owl's scientist henchmen created me as a means of summoning an asteroid to destroy the world. You see, dinosaurs like me have been blessed, some would say cursed, with an ability to trigger the End of the World when things aren't going right. I thought the world was fine, but the Owl wanted to use me to summon an asteroid against my will. But I stood up to him and beat up most of his cronies. He ended up fleeing to the Castle on the Hill and has been there observing the world ever since."

The baby's foot felt warm to Sheila's touch. To her surprise, it began to wiggle its legs and arms.

"Oh dear God!"

Sheila put her hands over her mouth.

"It's alive!"

As if in imitation of Sheila, the baby closed its frog eyes

and began to cry.

Its arms reached toward her.

Margaret wanted to be held.

"These days," Dan turned the page, "the Owl is looking for another way to destroy the world. He's already got a personal rocket ready to blast him into space if he ever achieves his goal. He believes that the creatures of this world weren't meant to exist: that we are nothing but molecular anomalies. He already has an entire universe inside his head which he controls every aspect of. He believes *that* universe is ideal, and therefore, the only one that matters.

"The pterodactyl you met was a test subject like me who got away. I survived, but she apparently didn't. I don't know where the safe containing her eggs is hidden. I've been searching this facility top-to-bottom for the past year trying to find it as well. I'm surprised you even made it here. You are the first creatures ever to visit me from outside. I commend you for finding the flute. That mouse is a slippery one. I can't believe you caught the little bugger."

"What clues do you have as to the safe's whereabouts?" asked Lily.

"The only info I've been able to gather after tearing this library/laboratory complex apart is that it has something to do with mirrors, probability, and electromagnetism. If one can synthesize these three ideas, an unused faculty of the brain will be unlocked, allowing the person to 'see' the safe in real space. That's all I've been able to put together by referencing and cross-referencing every book in this library."

"Thanks Mr. Diplodocus," Lily smiled a faint smile. "At least it's a start."

"Call me D. Plod or just D. That's probably what my friends would call me if I had any."

"Well, you do now." Lily extended her hand and D bumped it with his big flat foot.

"So, how do we start?" Abe said, feeling ignored.

"First," said Lily, "we've got to access the internet and scrutinize the crap out of all scientific topics in which mirrors, probability, and electromagnetism intermesh. We gotta do it before the Owl comes to poop on our party."

"Right," said Abe, repressing a groan."

After standing in shock for a full minute, Sheila discarded her inhibitions and scooped the infant out of its frozen casket.

"It's okay sweetie," she cooed. "I'll get you to your mommy, it's okay," she whispered softly, swaying Margaret back and forth.

The little girl smiled. She was a very cute froggie indeed.

The elevator dinged and the door slid open. They had arrived at the sub-sub basement.

The kids had finished the bag of candy hearts and the hospital staff was now passing out brownies on flimsy paper plates.

Dan licked his finger and turned another page.

"The frog, the lobster, and the diplodocus shielded their eyes as the light of artificial day blasted their corneas. The Owl would likely show up within a day's time. This estimate took into account every other project on the Owl's to-do list as governing body of the city. The three needed to work quickly. Hopefully the internet connection at the Weimaraner Café wasn't in one of its shoddy phases."

A nurse appeared in the doorway and pointed to her wristwatch, indicating that today's story session was at its end.

"I suppose we'll leave off there for today," Dan closed the book and placed it on the table next to him. "I hope you all can join me next time."

The children who had finished their brownies were shepherded out of the room and on to some other activity designed to keep their minds off their illnesses and the specter of chemo and radiation therapy.

Dan sighed and rubbed his eyebrows. *Where could Sheila be? That boy's frog couldn't have gone* that *far.*

Dan felt someone tap his shoulder. It was the thirteen-year-old with glasses.

"Mr. Z? Has your wife found Mr. Peepers yet?"

Dan felt the urge to chuckle, but his anxiety wouldn't let him.

"She must still be searching for him. This is a really big hospital and that frog can probably cover a lot of ground since he's so good at jumping. Why don't you come with me and we'll let security know about it."

"Please don't tell security!" The boy's eyes seemed ready to liquefy at any second. "They'll kill him for sure. He's a special frog. Just between you and me, he's a product of secret research. I swiped him from a lab at another hospital. I read in the files they had on him that he can live forever as long as he doesn't get hurt."

Dan bit his lip. *This kid might've grown up to be a great storyteller if he had the luxury of years ahead of him.*

"How about this, we'll have the nurse's station page my wife. It's very likely that she has found him already and is just lost. You can come with me if it's okay with the nurse here."

Dan glanced at the nurse and she nodded in approval.

"Alright, bud, let's find that frog."

The boy smiled and his eyes were now solid.

The first thing Sheila noticed when she got off the elevator was the door with a big '14' on it.

"Fourteen," she whispered. "Why does everything

always have to be associated with a number?" Her labored breaths formed plumes of white in the wet air of the hospital underworld. She pressed a button and the door slid open with a hiss. Margaret began to cry. Sheila froze for a second, then inched forward cautiously into whatever awaited her beyond.

After Dan and the boy had poked their heads into each of the rooms on that floor, they approached the nurse's station.

"Excuse me," Dan waved at a pretty nurse whose nose was bejeweled with a silver stud, "I can't seem to find my wife, would you mind paging her for–"

"Just hold on one second," the nurse lowered her gaze to the boy. "Jonathan, it's time to go to chemo. Deborah will take you." She indicated a suntanned nurse leaning against the wall. Deborah waved and flashed her pearly whites at the boy.

Jonathan gave Dan a look like his favorite stuffed animal had been tossed into a wood chipper.

"It's okay, pal." Dan put a hand on the boy's shoulder. "I'll find your frog. And if worse comes to worst, I'll see about getting you a new one."

Jonathan tore his gaze away from Dan and dragged his emaciated frame over to Deborah. He shot Dan one last glance before he and Deborah disappeared into the framework of the building/machine designed to keep human souls fettered to their bodies.

"Sorry about that, sir," the nurse behind the counter said, shuffling a stack of manila folders into order. "What was it you needed help with?"

Dan couldn't answer. Momentarily, he was gone from this world: focused intently on grinding a hole into the cold, hard floor with the ball of his foot.

· · ·

On the wall of Room 14 was a rack of translucent eggs wired to a supercomputer. Something about the eggs struck a vein in Sheila.

Margaret had calmed down and was pulling at strands of Sheila's hair.

"Seems like normal healthy baby behavior to me. Brain or not, this kid's got one strong grip."

She edged closer to the wall of eggs. She could feel her breast tissue quivering with each thud of her heart. She approached an egg at eye level labeled '475.'

The silhouette of a tiny hand groped at the wall of the egg. This confirmed Sheila's darkest suspicions. These eggs contained living Frogbabies. There were five hundred of them arranged in twenty five columns of twenty. Egg 475 had a name next to its number: 'Kerri-Lynn Slattery.'

"This can't be," Sheila gasped. "Is this Jamie Slattery's baby? The single mom who lives on our block who posted on Facebook about having a miscarriage?"

She scanned more of the names: "Smith, Adam. Smith, Christopher. Snelling, Julia? That's Molly Snelling's baby! The art teacher who also said she had a miscarriage. In fact, these are all names of people who have had miscarriages: Kim Falconi, Beth Andersen. Wait a minute."

While still holding Margaret, Sheila made a beeline for the lower right-hand corner of the wall where the 'Z' names would be. If there was a chance Ryan wasn't dead, she had to know.

Sure enough, egg number 500 was labeled 'Zebrowski, Ryan.'

It took all of Sheila's strength not to burst at the seams. Her baby was alive. She needed to get him out of here.

With Margaret in her left arm, she tore open the egg with her right. Salty liquid splashed onto the floor and pooled at her feet. Then she heard a sound sweeter than the most sublime orchestral piece. Ryan was crying. His arms reached toward her and his eyes glistened with longing. She pressed her cheek against his. The fact that he had been starved of his mother's love for more than a month made her feel sick inside.

"Let's go home," she whispered. She couldn't help staring into those magnificent eyes.

Ryan smiled, and Sheila smiled back despite her tears.

"Who's there?!" A man's voice rang out like rifle fire.

"It doesn't matter who's there." Her voice cracked the air like a whip.

Margaret started to cry. "I'm going home with my son and bringing Margaret back to her mother. There's nothing you can do about it. Will it kill him if I remove these wires?"

"Put the baby down!" It was a man in a casual suit whose wire-rimmed glasses reflected the piss-yellow of the eggs. Behind him was a battalion of security guards, and other men in suits.

"Back the fuck off!" Sheila inched as close to Ryan as she could. "What are you doing with these children? Why are you keeping them here? Why did you lie to their families about them being dead?"

"Okay, okay," said the man, "relax. I understand that you're upset. Any mother would be, and you have a right to be. But before you accuse us of being monsters, boogeymen, or what have you, I think you deserve to know why we kept your baby as well as all these others alive in secret."

"Save it for the courtroom you fucking swine. I don't have time for this shit. I'm going to introduce Ryan to his father and then I'm calling the police ..."

The man in the suit laughed, "Ma'am, we *are* the police."

Two men in black coveralls appeared behind Sheila. One stuck her left deltoid with a syringe and the other snatched Margaret. They hauled Sheila's limp body onto a gurney and wheeled her off to one of the sub-sub basement's holding rooms.

"We'll have to patch that unit with syntho-dermis until it heals," the man in the suit indicated Ryan's egg. He turned to face the entourage behind him. "This drill went better than I had hoped. As you saw, we're more than prepared to deal with intruders. The Video will set her mind straight and keep her from interfering any further. We'll inform the husband that she's been involved in an accident involving biologically hazardous material and that he can't see her because it would endanger his health. When we release her, she'll have a memory blackout spanning from her discovery of Room 14 to her release from this hospital. Project RIBBIT will remain unhindered, that much I can assure you."

When Sheila awoke, she was strapped to a chair. Her eyelids were being pried open by plastic spacers and every now and then, a hand would emerge from the shadows and squeeze droplets of saline solution into her eyes. She could wiggle her toes and open and close her hands, but her head was firmly held in place. A screen on the opposite wall lit up. A countdown like those featured in old movies began:

5 ... 4 ... 3 ... 2 ... 1 ...

A video began to play, the contents of which Sheila would never be able to consciously remember.

Don't Worry. Leave the Future to us. We won't be sad that you're not around. We've got ourselves, and that's all we need. The nothingness of Infinite Time will inch ever forward like a centipede in the dark. The candle glowing in the chapel may have been pretty to look at, but there was nothing to stumble upon in the first place. We will serve as

your legacy: complete and empty, the perfect form. All
prayers will be answered. AMEN.

Since August of 2001, the global think tank Project RIBBIT
had been working with corporations like Monsanto to alter
the human gene pool via chemical additives in foods and
beverages. The percentage of children born without brains
and spines spiked to ninety percent over the course of fifteen
years as a result. Most Frogbabies were not actually born
dead as their parents were led to believe. Many survived
with only a brainstem keeping their heart pumping. The
lack of a central nervous system or any other mental facul-
ties allowed them to live without ever experiencing physical
or emotional pain.

There was, however, a major difference between Frogbabies and those who became vegetables as a result of trau-
matic brain injuries. Accident victims often had access to
pleasurable and painful memories left over from before their
accident. These stored experiences made living in a vegetative state all the more unbearable. According to the Project
RIBBIT scientists, the life experience of a Frogbaby was the
ideal life experience; a vegetative state without prior knowledge of pain and pleasure.

After they were born, the babies were collected by
Project personnel and kept alive in secret laboratories. The
masterminds claimed there was no living thing more innocent and unbiased than a baby born without a brain. They
believed that the human tendency to erroneously organize
data gleaned from stimuli was the cause of the 'loss of innocence' described in the book of Genesis. To be born unable
to construct these meta-realities would be to remain in Eden
forever.

Even after the death of the last human, the Frogbabies

would continue to live hooked up to their synthetic wombs, floating in bliss, existing as a race incapable of worry and anxiety. They would be mankind's last and truest form. The apes that had invented fire, the wheel, and taxes would bow out gracefully and leave the world for the Frogbabies to inherit.

In the meantime, Project RIBBIT would learn all it could about how Frogbabies perceived the world by analyzing their sensory processes through computers interfaced with their brainstems. This data would be used to construct a simulacrum of Frogbaby consciousness called an Artificial Innocence. In the event that the Frogchildren's bodies were destroyed by natural disaster, rockets carrying copies of the Artificial Innocence would be blasted into space to seed the universe with purity and joy.

Ever since Sheila made contact with those 'hazardous chemicals' at the hospital, she hasn't been right in the head. Every night, she'd have the same dream:

She'd be naked and hovering above her bed in the fetal position while a frog in a lobster's body blew bubbles in the hallway. One of the bubbles would take the form of an analog computer. The bubble would wrap itself around the head of a diplodocus, connect to his brain and inform him that the safe he'd been searching for had been hidden in the nerve ganglion in his left hip the entire time. The frog-lobster would blow two more bubbles for himself and his female frog companion. Using their computer bubble helmets, the three of them would link their minds, unlock the safe and free the pterodactyl eggs trapped inside.

The eggs would hatch and the frog, lobster, and diplodocus would mount the baby pterodactyls and fly up to a castle in the mountains. Once there, the pterodactyls would peck out the panoptic eyes of an Owl King too busy crunching numbers to notice that his kingdom had collapsed.

The lobster, frog, and diplodocus would look at each other thinking *now what?*

After gorging on the innards of the Owl, the pterodactyls, still hunched over their kill, would crane their heads toward the three heroes. Ropes of saliva would be dangling from their bloody jaws and their eyes would be glistening with hunger.

"I don't like the look of this," the frog would say.

"Let's get out of here!" The lobster would climb on the frog's back and the frog would jump out the window.

"Wait for me!" The diplodocus would shout, but it would be too late. The sounds of his being eaten would reverberate off the hills for all to hear.

The frog and lobster would return to where their pond was supposed to be, but in its place would be a strip mall with a video store, fortune-teller shop, and a dealer of Native Mazguanian crafts.

When Sheila woke, she'd feel as though a crucial piece of information was missing from her brain. Whenever she thought about Ryan or Frogbabies, her head would start hurting and her train of thought would be rerouted to complacency. Exhausted from trying to remember something she never knew, she'd resign herself to acceptance. The Frogbabies' lives were blissfully short, and that's the way it was. Ryan had been born into a state of pure Zen. It would be downright selfish of her to make him stay in this world just to satisfy her nurturing instinct. Eventually, she and everybody else would enter the same realm of nothingness. Until then, she'd just have to endure the ups and downs of life and the dreams that screamed at her every night, telling her that something wasn't right.

ACKNOWLEDGMENTS

If not for the following people, this book would not have been possible: Mom and Dad, Professors Hollis Seamon, Barbara Ungar, Daniel Nester, Rone Shavers, Alyssa Colton and all other members of the College of Saint Rose English Department faculty who inspired me, Librarian Katherine Moss, Josh Smith at Bedlam Publishing, Leza Cantoral and Christoph Paul at CLASH Books, Lev Cantoral (for designing the cover,) Amanda McDowell, everyone at Albany Poets for giving me a platform and supporting me, the editors of the journals, magazines and anthologies who published my work, anyone who bought this book or came to see me read, the Tarot (my personal conduit to the wisdom of the Universe,) and all those writers, artists, animators, filmmakers, musicians, and game developers who help keep the wheels of my brain turning on a daily basis: THANK YOU!

Brett Petersen is a writer, musician and artist from Albany, New York, whose high-functioning autism only enhances his creativity. He earned his B.A. in English from the College of Saint Rose in 2011, and since then, his stories and poems have appeared in over a dozen print and online publications. *The Parasite From Proto Space and Other Stories* is his first book, and unless he is apprehended by the Trump Regime for being an outspoken autistic, will certainly not be his last. Academic critics should note that the subject matter of his stories and his taste in literature in general was heavily inspired by Japanese role-playing video games such as Xenogears, Chrono Trigger, and Shin Megami Tensei. Aside from his writing career, he is the rhythm guitarist and vocalist for sludge rock band Raziel's Tree, a competent visual artist, Tarot reader, and wannabe Kabbalist. All things Brett Petersen can be found at http://www.jellyfishentity.wordpress.com.

ALSO BY CLASH BOOKS

TRAGEDY QUEENS: STORIES INSPIRED BY LANA DEL REY & SYLVIA PLATH

Edited by Leza Cantoral

GIRL LIKE A BOMB

Autumn Christian

CENOTE CITY

Monique Quintana

99 POEMS TO CURE WHATEVER'S WRONG WITH YOU OR CREATE THE PROBLEMS YOU NEED

Sam Pink

THIS BOOK IS BROUGHT TO YOU BY MY STUDENT LOANS

Megan J. Kaleita

PAPI DOESN'T LOVE ME NO MORE

Anna Suarez

ARSENAL/SIN DOCUMENTOS

Francesco Levato

THIS IS A HORROR BOOK

Charles Austin Muir

WE PUT THE LIT IN LITERARY

CL◀SH

CLASHBOOKS.COM

FOLLOW US ON TWITTER, IG & FB

@clashbooks

EMAIL US

clashmediabooks@gmail.com

Printed in the USA
CPSIA information can be obtained
at www.ICGtesting.com
JSHW082343140824
68134JS00020B/1858